**Francis still didn't understand
what had happened.**

One minute she'd been looking up at the
night sky, searching for the tail star of the Big
Dipper. The next minute she'd felt someone
put an arm around the small of her back. She
hadn't even been able to turn around and see
who it was before another arm went behind
her knees and she was lifted up.

Suddenly, instead of the night sky, she was
looking square into the face of Flint Harris.
For a second she couldn't breathe. Her mind
went blank. Surely it could not be Flint. Not
her Flint. She blinked. He was still there.

Oh, my Lord, she suddenly realized. It's true.
And he's kidnapping me!

Books by Janet Tronstad

Love Inspired

*An Angel for Dry Creek #81
*A Gentleman for Dry Creek #110
*A Bride for Dry Creek #138

*Dry Creek

JANET TRONSTAD

grew up on a small farm in central Montana. One of her favorite things to do was to visit her grandfather's bookshelves, where he had a large collection of Zane Grey novels. She's always loved a good story.

Today Janet lives in Pasadena, California, where she works in the research department of a medical organization. In addition to writing novels, she researches and writes nonfiction magazine articles.

A Bride for Dry Creek
Janet Tronstad

Published by Steeple Hill Books™

STEEPLE HILL BOOKS

Steeple
Hill™

ISBN 0-373-87145-7

A BRIDE FOR DRY CREEK

Copyright © 2001 by Janet Tronstad

Visit us at www.steeplehill.com

Printed in U.S.A.

Set me as a seal upon thine heart,
as a seal upon thine arm: for love is strong as
death.... Many waters cannot quench love,
neither can the floods drown it....
                    —*Song of Solomon* 8:6-7

Dedicated with love
To my two brothers and their wives
Ralph and Karen Tronstad
Russell and Heidi Tronstad
May God be with all of you
Now and forevermore.

Chapter One

A single fly buzzed past Francis Elkton and swooped up to the bare lights that hung from the rafters of the old barn. Francis didn't notice the fly, but on most nights she would have even though her eyes were now half-closed as she slow danced to an old fifties tune.

Francis was an immaculate housekeeper. And a first-class manager. She often said, in her job with the City of Denver, that the two went hand in hand. You only needed to look in someone's top desk drawer, she'd say, to predict what kind of a city manager they would be. Whether it was paper clips or people or drainage pipes, everything needed an order.

She would never have tolerated an out-of-place fly if she hadn't been so distracted.

But tonight, the fly was only one more guest at the wedding reception, and Francis was too busy trying to keep her unwanted memories in their place to give any attention to the proper place of a mere insect. Every time she opened her eyes she realized that things were not turning out the way she had planned.

She'd taken a three-month leave from her job and come back to Dry Creek, Montana, because she thought she'd be able to stand up to her past—to look her memories of Flint L. Harris square in the eye—and be free of him once and for all. She was mentally cleaning out her files, she told herself. Throwing away outdated papers. Putting her life back in order even if it had taken her twenty years to face the task.

The only reason she'd decided to do it now was that Sam Goodman, her neighbor in Denver, had said he would not wait forever to marry her. She'd realized suddenly that she could not give her heart to Sam, or any other man, until she got it completely back from Flint.

It had been a sentimental decision to come back to Dry Creek to purge herself. She reasoned that the memories had started here in this ranching community, in the shadows of the Big Sheep Mountains. And they would surely end here if she just screwed up her mind and willed them to be gone. It was like reaching deep inside herself to pull out the roots of an unwanted weed that had refused to die over the years.

But, for the first time since she'd come back, she realized her heart wasn't bending to her will. The past had not grown dimmer because she'd stood up to it. No, the past was right here before her in living color whether she wanted to see it or not.

The pink crepe paper streamers coming down from the rafters were the same color her high school class had used twenty years ago for their prom. Back then her classmates had gone to Miles City to school and had decorated the gym there with their streamers.

Tonight, the dance was being held in the large old barn her brother Garth had built for loading cattle. He had not used the barn for his cattle for several years now, and the community of Dry Creek had scrubbed it clean for their annual Christmas pageant some months ago. On a cold winter night like tonight, the inside of the barn shone bright and the windows were covered with frost.

Dry Creek was fast making the barn into an informal center for all kinds of occasions. Like tonight's dance to celebrate the wedding of Glory Becker and Matthew Curtis. The dance wasn't a prom, but the music was the same. The same swaying music. The same soft laughter of other couples in the background.

Francis could close her eyes and almost imagine

it was Flint who held her in his arms. Flint with his shy halting gladness to see her and the tall wiry length of his twenty-year-old body. Even back then, she should have known that dancing with him would come to no good

"Francis?" A slightly alarmed man's voice growled in her right ear.

Francis blinked and then blushed. Jess, one of her brother's older ranch hands, had invited her to dance, and it was his face that now looked at her suspiciously. She hadn't realized until he spoke that her arms had crept up his back until she had him in an embrace that was more than friendly. She shook the memories from her eyes, cleared her throat and loosened her arms. "Sorry."

"That's okay." Jess ducked his head, apparently reassured once the sensible Francis was back. Then he added teasingly, "After all, your brother did tell me to stick close to you tonight."

"He's not still worried about that phone call?" Francis gladly diverted the conversation to her brother's needless caution. "Just because some guy calls up and says someone might be out to kidnap me—it's all nonsense anyway. Even if Garth did know something about the rustlers who have been hitting this area—which he doesn't—well, it doesn't make sense. Before they start making any threats, these rustlers should find out if Garth knows anything that's a danger to them. Any manager would tell them that's the first step. They might be criminals, but that's no excuse for sloppy planning. You need to identify your problem and then verify how big it is before you can even hope to solve it."

"Way I hear it, it wasn't just some guy that called."

Apparently Jess only heard the first part of what she'd said. Francis had noticed that the ranch hands who worked for her brother tended to let their eyes glaze over when she tried to teach them management techniques.

"The man never gave his name," Francis corrected stiffly.

"Didn't need to from the way I heard it," Jess mumbled. "Begging your pardon for mentioning him. Still—can't be too careful."

No wonder she was having so much trouble getting rid of her memories of Flint, Francis thought. He seemed to have more lives than a stray alley cat. She'd bury him one day and he'd be resurrected the next. Did everyone in Dry Creek know about that phone call?

"I don't believe it was Flint Harris on the other end of that phone call. For pity's sake—he probably doesn't even remember Dry Creek." *Lord knows he doesn't remember me*, Francis added silently. "He never had roots in Dry Creek. He only came here that one spring because his grandmother was ill. He hasn't been back since she died."

"Hasn't sold her place yet, though," Jess argued. "Even pays taxes on it. That's got to mean something."

"It means that it isn't worth selling. Who would buy it? The windows are all broken out and it's only got five acres with it. The only thing you could raise there is chickens and with the low price of eggs these days—"

Francis stopped herself. She didn't need to be her own worst enemy. She needed to forget chickens. That had been their adolescent dream—that they would live with his grandmother and make their living by selling eggs. A fool's dream. Even back then, it wouldn't have kept them in jeans and tennis shoes. She cleared her throat. "The point is that Flint Harris is nowhere near here."

"Like I said, I'm sorry to bring the louse up. If I'd have been here back then and met the boy, I'd have given him a good speaking to—treating a nice girl like you that way."

Francis stopped dancing and looked at Jess. He seemed to expect a response. "Well, thank you, but that wouldn't have been necessary. I could take care of myself even back then."

"If you say so."

Francis looked at him carefully. There it was. A steady gleam of pity in his eyes.

"Those rumors are not true." Francis bristled. The one thing she didn't miss in Denver was the gossip that flowed freely in a small community. "While it is true that he and I drove to Las Vegas after the prom and looked for a justice of the peace, it is not true that we were actually married."

"Mrs. Hargrove says—"

"Mrs. Hargrove wasn't there. I was. The man was not a justice of the peace. My father called down there and asked. They had no justice of the peace by that name. It doesn't matter what words we said, those papers we signed were worthless."

"You signed some papers?" The pity left his eyes. It was replaced by astonishment. "You still have them?"

"I didn't say I have papers," Francis said patiently. The last time she'd seen those papers, Flint had had them. She remembered the way he had carefully folded them and put them in his coat pocket. She hadn't realized at the time that any young bride with any sense asks to keep the papers herself—especially when the wedding takes place in Las Vegas. That should have been her first clue.

"Besides, that is long ago and done with," Francis said briskly. "As Mrs. Hargrove probably told you, even if it had been a marriage, it would have been the shortest marriage ever on record in Dry Creek—probably the shortest in all of Montana. I don't even think it lasted forty hours. We had the trip back from Vegas and then he dropped me off at my dad's to pack. Said he was going to Miles

City to buy me some roses—every bride needed roses, he said—those were the last words I ever heard from him. He never came back.''

Francis believed in slicing through her pain quickly and efficiently with a minimum of fuss. She'd held her breath when she recited the facts of those two days with Flint and now she let it out slowly. "I'm sure it was one of the smoothest exit lines in the book and I fell for it. Five weeks later I made arrangements to graduate early from high school and I left for Denver. That's all there was to it."

"But no one knew," Jess reproached her softly. "That's the only reason the folks here still remember it. No one but your father knew and then you just left so suddenly. These were your neighbors and friends. They cared about you, they just didn't know what was happening. Even now Mrs. Hargrove keeps trying to think back to something she could have said to make it better in those days for you— blames herself for not taking a more motherly role in your life—what with just you and your dad out there alone when Garth was in the service—keeps having this notion that Flint did come back in around that time and stopped at her place to ask for you."

"She's confused," Francis said flatly. People meant well, but it didn't help to sugarcoat the truth. "If he'd tried to find me, he'd have tried my father's place. He knew where it was. He'd been there enough times.''

''I suppose you're right.''

The dance ended and suddenly Francis felt foolish to be standing there arguing about whether or not a man had stopped to see her neighbor twenty years ago. ''I think I'll sit the next one out if it's all the same to you. You can tell my brother I'll be fine. I'll just be taking a rest.''

Jess looked relieved. ''I could use a break myself. My arthritis is acting up some.''

''Well, why didn't you say so? We could have sat the last two dances out—no need to be up and moving around on a cold night like this.''

''It is a blistering one out tonight, isn't it?''

''All the more reason to forget about the kidnapping threat,'' Francis agreed. ''No one but a fool would be out setting a trap tonight. It's too cold. No, I think the kids are right when they said it was that rival gang they have in Seattle calling to make mischief.''

Francis's brother, Garth, had offered the use of his ranch to a woman who ran a youth center for gang kids in Seattle. At the moment, thirty of the kids were learning to be better citizens by spending a few weeks in Dry Creek, Montana. Garth had been in charge of teaching the boys how to be gentlemen, and Francis had been astonished at his patience. He'd had them out in the barn practicing how to dip and twirl their dance partners, and the boys had loved it.

A rich society woman from Seattle, Mrs. Buckwalter, was underwriting the cost of the trip to Montana, and Francis couldn't help but notice how excited the older woman was tonight. Mrs. Buckwalter couldn't have been prouder of the teens if she'd given birth to every one of them.

And Francis couldn't blame her. The teenagers sparkled at this dance, the boys in their rented tuxedos and the girls in the old fifties prom dresses they'd borrowed from the women of Dry Creek. It was hard to believe that they were members of various gangs in Seattle. A few dance lessons and a sprinkling of ties and taffeta had transformed them.

"That's really the logical explanation," Francis concluded. If the other gang could only see the youth center kids now. She couldn't help but think they'd be a little jealous of the good time these kids were having.

"Maybe." Jess didn't look convinced. "Just don't take any unnecessary risks—your brother will have my hide. He's worried, you know—"

"Even if Flint did kidnap me, he'd never hurt me—no matter what Garth worries about." As Francis listened to herself saying the words, she realized how naive she sounded. She didn't know what kind of a man Flint might be today. She'd often wondered.

Jess looked at her. "Still, things happen."

"What could happen?" Francis waved her arms around. She might not know about Flint, but she did know about the people of Dry Creek. At least a hundred people were in the barn, some sitting on folding chairs along the two sides, a few standing by the refreshment table and dozens of them on the floor poised ready to dance to the next tune. A lot of muscle rested beneath the suits that had been unearthed for this party. "One little scream and fifty men would come to my rescue. I'm surrounded by Dry Creek. There isn't a safer place in all the world for me."

Jess grunted. "I guess you're right. Maybe you should go visit with Mrs. Hargrove a bit. Talk to those two little boys that belong to Matthew Curtis. Find out how they like the idea of having a new mama."

Francis smiled. She was fond of the four-year-old twins and liked to see them so happy. "Everyone knows how they feel about that. She's their angel. If their dad wasn't going to marry Glory, I think they'd wait and marry her themselves."

Meanwhile, outside in the dark...

Flint watched a fly buzz up to the headlight of the old cattle truck. Now, what was a fly doing in the middle of a Montana winter night so cold a man's nose hairs were likely to freeze?

Flint slid into the niche between two cars and hunched down in his black leather jacket. The worthless jacket was nearly stiff. That fly didn't belong here any more than Flint and his jacket did. He would bet the fly had made the mistake of crawling into that cattle truck when it'd been parked someplace a lot warmer. Say Seattle. Or San Francisco.

Even a rookie FBI agent would make the connection that the truck didn't belong to anyone local. And Flint had been with the Bureau for twenty years. No, the truck had to belong to the three men he'd identified as cattle thieves. He'd call in their location just as soon as he had something more concrete to tell the inspector than that he'd listened to them talk enough to know they were brothers.

The last time he'd made his daily check-in call, one of the guys had said the inspector was grumbling about him being out here on this assignment without a partner. Flint told him he had a partner—an ornery horse named Honey.

The fly made another pass close to Flint's face, seeking the warmth of his breath.

Flint half-cursed as he waved the fly away. He didn't need the fly to distract him from the mumbled conversation of the three men. They'd been standing in front of the cattle truck arguing for several minutes about some orders their boss had given to deliver a package.

Flint sure hoped they were talking about which cattle to steal next.

If not, that probably meant his tip was accurate and they were planning to kidnap Francis Elkton. He hoped Garth had taken the phone call he had made seriously and was keeping Francis inside, in some controlled area with no one but the good ladies of Dry Creek around her.

Flint envied all of the people of Dry Creek the heat inside the barn. The warmest he was likely to get anytime soon was when he went to feed Honey some oats.

It hadn't taken him more than a half hour on Honey's back to realize that her owner must have had a chuckle or two when he named her. She was more sour than sweet. Still, Flint rubbed his gloved hands over his arms and shivered. Honey might be a pain, but he missed her all the same. She was the only breathing thing he'd talked to since he came to Montana.

By now Honey would be wondering when they'd go home. When he'd ridden her to town tonight, he'd tied her reins to a metal clothesline pole in a vacant lot behind Mr. Gossett's house. The pole was out of the wind, but Honey would still be anxious for warmer quarters. Last night, he'd bedded her down in an abandoned chicken coop that still stood on the farm he'd inherited from his grandmother when she died fifteen years ago. As far as he knew, no one but gophers ever visited the place anymore.

He was half-surprised the men hiding by that cattle truck didn't use horses. The terrain on the south slopes of the Big Sheep Mountain Range wasn't steep, but it also wasn't paved. There were more fences than roads. The long, winding strings of barbed wire and aging posts did little in winter except collect snowdrifts. Flint had followed a dozen of those fences to reacquaint himself with the area last night and didn't see anything more than a thick-coated coyote or two.

But then these men probably didn't know how to ride a horse. Which meant they weren't professionals. If they had been pros, they would have learned before heading out here on a job like this. A pro would realize a horse would be a good escape option if the roads were blocked. Yes, a pro would learn to ride. Even if he needed to learn on a bad-tempered horse like Honey.

Flint's observations of the men had already made him suspect that they were not career kidnappers. They were too careless and disorganized to have lived long if they made a habit of breaking the law. But Flint knew that the crime syndicates liked to use amateurs for some jobs—they made good fall guys when things went sour.

Granted, the Boss—and the Bureau didn't know

who he was yet—had other reasons to use amateurs here. A pro would look so out of place in this rural community he might as well wear a red neon sticker that said Hired Killer—Arrest Me Now.

The fact that the men were too tender to ride horses made Flint hope that they would give it up for tonight and go home. The night was clear—there was enough moonlight so that Flint could see the low mountains that made up the Big Sheep Mountain Range. But it was ice-cracking cold and not getting any warmer.

The little town of Dry Creek stood a few miles off Interstate 94, which ran along the southern third of Montana from Billings on through Miles City. The town was nothing more than a few wood frame houses, an old square church, a café called Jazz and Pasta that was run by a young engaged couple, and a hardware store with a stovepipe sticking up through the roof. The pipe promised some kind of heat inside. Flint had not gone in to find out if the old Franklin stove he remembered was still being used. He hadn't even tried to find an opening in the frost so he could look in the window.

The memories Flint had of his days in Dry Creek were wrinkled by time, and he couldn't be sure if all the details like the Franklin stove were true or if he'd romanticized them over the years, mixing them up with some old-fashioned movie he'd seen or some nostalgic dream he'd had.

He realized he didn't want to know about the stove so he hadn't looked inside the hardware store.

Flint had only spent a few months in Dry Creek, but this little community—more than anywhere else on earth—was the place he thought of as home. His grandmother had lived her life here, and this is where he'd known Francis. The combination of the two would make this forever home to him.

None of the chrome-and-plastic-furnished apartments he'd rented over the years could even begin to compete. They were little more than closets to keep his clothes out of the rain. He couldn't remember the last time he'd cooked anything but coffee in any of them. No, none of them could compete with the homes around Dry Creek.

Even old man Gossett's place looked as though it had a garden of sorts—a few rhubarb stalks stuck up out of a snowdrift, and there was a crab apple tree just left of his back porch. There were no leaves on the tree, but Flint recognized the graceful swoop of the bare branches.

The trash barrel that the man kept in the vacant lot had a broken jelly jar inside. Flint suspected someone was making jelly from the apples that came off the tree. It might even be the old man.

Flint envied the old man his jelly and Flint didn't even like jelly. The jelly just symbolized home and community for him, and Flint felt more alone than he had for years. Maybe when he finished this business in Dry Creek, he should think about getting married.

That woman he'd started dating—Annette—he wondered if she could make apple jelly. He'd have to find out—maybe he should even send her a postcard. Women liked postcards. He hadn't seen any that featured Dry Creek, but maybe he'd stop in Billings when this was all over. Get her something with those mountains on it. In the daylight the Big Sheep Mountain Range was low and buff-colored with lots of dry sage in the foreground. Looked like a Zane Grey novel. Yes, a postcard was a good idea. That's what he'd do when this was all over.

From the sounds of the ruckus inside that old barn, the whole community of Dry Creek, Montana, was celebrating tonight. All eighty-five adults and the usual assortment of children.

Flint had checked the vital statistics before he headed down here. The place didn't have any more people now than it had had that spring he'd spent at his grandmother's place. The only new people that had come to the community were the busload of Seattle teenagers who were there for a month to see that all of life wasn't limited to the city streets. As long as Francis stayed with the people inside the barn, she would be safe.

That thought had no sooner crossed his mind than the side barn door opened. A woman stood silhouetted in the golden light from inside the barn. Flint felt all breath leave his body. It was Francis.

Francis let the winter air cool her. The ruby red material of her dress was thin, but it had still suddenly gotten much too hot inside the barn. The rumor that Flint had been the one who made the phone call to Garth this afternoon had opened up all of the speculation about her and Flint. She saw it in the eyes of her neighbors. They were asking themselves why she'd never married, why she'd moved away so quickly all those years ago, why she'd never come back to live in Dry Creek until now—why, why, why. The questions would be endless until they'd worried her heart to a bone.

She only wished the asking of the questions would help her find an answer, she thought ruefully. Because, even if no one else had been asking those questions, she would be asking them.

But not tonight, she decided. Tonight she would just breathe the crisp night air and look at the stars that were scattered across the sky like pieces of glitter sprinkled over velvet. She used to love to go out on a winter's night like this and find the Big Dipper.

Now where is it, she asked herself as she stepped through the open door and outside. The barn was hiding the constellation from her. But if she went over by that old cattle truck she could see it.

She suddenly realized she hadn't gone looking for the Big Dipper in many years.

Flint swore. No wonder being a hero had gone out of style. His leg still stung where Francis had kicked him in her glittery high-heeled shoes, and one of his toes could well be broken where she had stomped on it.

Next time, he'd let the kidnappers have her. She was more than a match for most of the hired toughs he'd seen in his time. She'd certainly hold her own with the men in the cattle truck.

And thinking of his toes, what was she doing with shoes like that, anyway? Women only wore shoes like that to please a man. That meant she must have a boyfriend inside that old barn. That was one statistic he hadn't thought to check before heading out here.

Flint's only consolation was that his horse seemed to know he needed her and was behaving for once.

"Now I know why they call you Honey," Flint murmured encouragingly as he nudged his horse down the dark road.

"Hargh." An angry growl came from the bundle behind him, but Flint didn't even look back. Except for being temporarily gagged, Francis was doing better than he was. He'd even tied his jacket around her. Not that she had thanked him for it.

"Yes, sir, you're a sweetie, all right," Flint continued quietly guiding his horse. Honey knew the way home even if it was only a humble abandoned shed. That horse could teach some people the meaning of gratitude.

Or, if not gratitude, at least cooperation, Flint fumed.

If it wasn't for his years of training as an agent, Flint would have turned around and told Francis a thing or two. What did she think?

There was no time for niceties when he knew those two hired thugs were waiting for Francis. He'd heard them repeat their instructions about kidnapping Garth's sister in her black jacket with the old high school emblem of a lion.

Early on in the evening, the two men made a decision to wait for her by the bus—parked right next to that old cattle truck they'd come in. They hoped Francis would tire of dancing and come to sit in the bus. Flint had winced when he heard the plan. The two men were clearly amateurs, unfamiliar with Montana. No one, no matter how tired, would come to rest in a cold bus when the engine wasn't running.

But he saw their dilemma. They couldn't face down the whole town of Dry Creek or even the busload of kids that would be going back to the Elkton ranch. That's why he wasn't surprised, after the men had waited a few hours and gotten thoroughly cold themselves, to hear them start talking about going home and waiting until the next day to kidnap Francis.

Flint was hoping they'd leave soon. And they would have, except who should come outside for a late night stroll but Francis. She wasn't wearing the black jacket, but Flint couldn't risk the thugs getting a close look at her and realizing who she was, even without the jacket.

There was no time for fancy plans. The only way to protect Francis was to grab her first and worry about the men later.

Flint knew the men might be a problem if they realized what he was doing, but he hadn't counted on Francis's resistance. He thought once she knew it was him she'd come quietly. Perhaps even gratefully. But the moment he saw recognition dawn, she fought him like he was her worst enemy. He hadn't planned on gagging her until she made it clear she was going to scream.

And all the while she was kicking and spitting, he'd been doing her a great service.

Yes, he sighed, he could see why being a hero had gone completely out of style. It wasn't easy being the knight on the shining white horse. Not with the women of today. Come to think of it, it wasn't even easy with the horses of today. Honey made it clear she'd rather be eating oats than rescuing a damsel in distress.

"Tired, that's what you are," Flint said softly as

he leaned over the horse's neck. Honey sighed, and he gave the horse another encouraging nudge. "We're both tired, aren't we? But don't worry. We're almost there. Then I'll have something sweet for you."

The bundle behind him gave an indignant gasp and then another angry growl.

"I was talking to the horse." Flint smiled in spite of himself.

Chapter Two

Francis wished she had worn those ruby silk flowers in her hair like the teenagers had urged her to do. At least then, when the horse shook her, the petals would fall to the ground and leave a trail in the snow for someone to follow when they searched for her in the morning. Maybe if she were lucky, some of the sequins on her long evening dress would fall to the ground and leave a trail of reddish sparkles.

She still didn't understand what had happened.

One minute she'd been looking at the night sky, searching for the tail star of the Big Dipper. The next minute she'd felt someone put an arm around the small of her back. She hadn't even been able to turn around and see who it was before another arm went behind her knees and she was lifted up.

Suddenly, instead of seeing the night sky she was looking square into the face of Flint Harris. For a second, she couldn't breathe. Her mind went blank. Surely, it could not be Flint. Not her Flint. She blinked. He was still there.

She was speechless. He was older, it was true. Instead of the smooth-skinned boy she remembered, she saw the face of a man. Weather had etched a few fine lines around his eyes. A tiny scar crossed the left side of his chin. His face was fuller, stronger.

Oh, my Lord, she suddenly realized. *It's true. He's kidnapping me!*

Francis opened her mouth to scream. Nothing came out. She took a good breath to try again when Flint swore and hurriedly stuffed an old bandanna into her mouth. The wretched piece of cloth smelled of horse. She understood why it smelled when Flint slung her over his back like she was nothing to him but a sack of potatoes in a fancy bag. He then hauled her off to a horse tied behind Mr. Gossett's house.

Once Flint got to the horse, he stopped to slip some wool mittens from his hands and onto her hands. The mittens were warm inside from his body heat, and the minute he slid them onto her hands, her fingers felt like they were being tucked under a quilt.

But she didn't have time to enjoy it.

There was a light on in old man Gossett's house, and Francis struggled to scream through her gag.

She knew the man was home since he never went to community gatherings. He was a sour old man and she wasn't sure he'd help her even if he knew she was in trouble. Through the thin curtains on his window, she saw him slowly walking around inside his kitchen. Unless he'd grown deaf in these past years, he must have heard her. If he did, he didn't come outside to investigate.

Flint didn't give her a second chance to scream. He threw her over the back of the horse, slapped his jacket on her shoulders and mounted up.

Ever since then she'd been bouncing along, face-down, behind his saddle.

Finally, the horse stopped.

They had entered a grove of pine trees. The night was dark, but the moon was out. Inside the grove, the trees cut off the light of the moon, as well. Only a few patches of snow were visible. From the sounds beneath the horse's hoofs, the rest of the ground was covered with dried pine needles.

The saddle creaked as Flint stood to dismount.

Francis braced herself. She'd been trained to cope with hostage situations in her job and knew a person was supposed to cooperate with the kidnapper. But surely that didn't apply to criminals one knew. She and this particular criminal had slow danced together. He couldn't shoot her.

She'd already decided to wait her chance and escape. She had a plan. Flint had made a mistake in putting the mittens on her. The wool of the mittens kept the cord from gripping her wrists tightly. When Flint stepped down on the ground, she would loosen the tie on her wrists, swing her body around and nudge that horse of his into as much of a gallop as the poor thing could handle.

Flint stepped down.

The horse whinnied in protest.

"What the—" Flint turned and started to swear.

Francis had her leg caught around the horn of the saddle. She'd almost made the turn. But almost wasn't enough. She was hanging, with one leg behind the back of the saddle and one hooked around the horn. She'd ripped the skirt of her ruby sheath dress and all she'd accomplished was a change of view. Her face was no longer looking at the ground. Instead, she was looking straight into the astonished eyes of Flint L. Harris.

Francis groaned into her gag. She'd also twisted a muscle in her leg.

And she'd spooked the horse. The poor thing was prancing like a boxer. Each move of the beast's hooves sent a new pain through Francis's leg.

"Easy, Honey," Flint said soothingly as he reached out to touch the horse.

Francis saw his hands in the dark. His rhythm was steady, and he stroked the animal until she had quieted.

"Atta girl." Flint gave the horse one last long stroke.

Flint almost swore again. They should outlaw high heels. How was a man supposed to keep his mind on excitable horses and bad guys when right there—just a half arm's length away—was a dainty ankle in a strappy red high heel? Not to mention a leg that showed all the way up to the thigh because of the tear in that red dress. He was glad it was dark. He hoped Francis couldn't see in his eyes the thoughts that his mind was thinking.

"She'll be quiet now." Flint continued speaking slow and calm for the horse's benefit. "But she spooks easy. Try to stay still."

Even in the darkness inside the pine grove he could see the delicate lines of Francis's face behind the gag. Her jaw was clenched tight. He hadn't realized—

"I know it's not easy," he added softly. "I didn't mean to frighten you."

A muffled protest came from behind the gag.

Francis had worn her dark hair loose, and it spilled into his hands when he reached up to untie the gag. Flint's hands were cold, and her hair whispered across them like a warm summer breeze. He couldn't resist lingering a moment longer than necessary inside the warmth of her hair.

"It's not how I meant to say hello again," Flint said as he untied the bandanna. And it was true.

What he'd say when he met Francis again had gone from being a torture to a favorite game with him over the years. None of his fantasies of the moment had involved her looking at him with eyes wide with fear.

"Don't pretend you ever meant to see me again." Francis spit the words out when the gag was finally gone. Her voice was rusty and bitter even to her own ears. "Not that it matters," she quickly lied. "I—"

Francis stopped. She almost wished she had the gag in her mouth.

"That was a long time ago," Francis finally managed.

"Yes, it was," Flint agreed as he finished unraveling the cord he'd used to tie Francis's hands behind her. It might seem like a long time ago to her. To him it was yesterday.

"Cold night out," Flint added conversationally as he stuffed the cord into his pocket. He needed to move their words to neutral territory. Her wrists had been as smooth as marble. "Is it always this cold around here in February?"

"It used to be," Francis answered. She'd felt Flint's fingertips on the skin of her wrists just at the top of her mittens. His fingers were ice cold. For the first time, she realized the mittens on her hands must have been the only ones he had. "Folks say, though, that the winters lately have been mild."

"That's right, you don't live here anymore, do

you?'' Flint asked as he put his hand on Francis's lower leg. He felt her stiffen. "Easy. Just going to try and unravel you here without scaring Honey."

Flint let his hand stay on Francis's leg until both his hand and that section of her leg were warm. He let his hand massage that little bit of leg ever so slightly so it wouldn't stiffen up. "Don't want to make you pull the muscle in that leg any more than it looks like you've already done."

Flint had to stop his hand before it betrayed him. Francis was wearing real nylon stockings. The ones like they used to make. A man's hands slid over them like they were cream. If Flint were a betting man, he would bet nylon like this didn't come from panty hose, either. No, she was wearing the old-fashioned kind of nylons with a garter belt.

This knowledge turned him first hot then cold. A woman only wore those kind of stockings for one reason.

"You won't be dancing any time soon," he offered with deceptive mildness as he pressed his hands against his thighs to warm them enough to continue. "So I suppose that boyfriend of yours will just have to be patient."

"He has been," Francis said confidently. "Thank you for reminding me."

Francis thought of Sam Goodman. He might not make her blood race, but he didn't make it turn to ice, either. He was a good, steady man. A man she'd be proud to call her boyfriend. Maybe even her husband. She almost wished she'd encouraged him more when he'd called last week and offered to come for a visit.

Flint pressed his lips together. He should have thought about the boyfriend before he took off with Francis like he had. It had already occurred to him that he could have simply returned her to the good people of Dry Creek. Instead of heading for the horse, he could have headed for the light streaming out the open barn door and simply placed her inside. If it had been anyone but Francis, he would have.

But Francis addled his brain. All he could think of was keeping her safe, and he didn't trust anyone else—not even some fancy boyfriend who made her want to dress in garters and sequins—to get her far enough away from the rustlers. He had to make sure she was safe or to take a bullet for her if something happened and those two kidnappers got spooked.

Still, a boyfriend could pose problems. "I suppose he'll be wondering where you are," Flint worried aloud as he slowly turned the saddle to allow Francis's leg to tip toward him.

Francis stared in dismay. Flint was helping her untangle herself, but he was obviously positioning her so that she would slide off the back of the horse and into his arms.

"I can walk," Francis said abruptly.

"You'd have better luck flying at the moment,"

Flint said as he put a hand on each of her hips and braced himself. "Put your arms around my neck and I'll swing you around."

"I don't think—" Francis began. Flint's hands swept past her hips and wrapped themselves around her waist. She took a quick, involuntary breath. Surely he could feel her heart pounding inside her body. The material on this wretched dress the girls had talked her into wearing was not at all good for this sort of thing. It was much too thin. She could feel the heat from Flint's hands as he cradled her waist.

"You don't need to think—just move with me," Flint directed. He couldn't take much more of this.

It must be the cold that made his hands even more sensitive than usual. He not only felt every ridge of beaded sequin on the dress, he felt every move of her muscles beneath the palm of his hands. He knew she was trying to pull herself away from him. That she was struggling to move her leg without his help. The knowledge didn't do much for a man's confidence. He remembered the days when she used to want him to hold her.

"You're going to scare the horse," Flint cautioned softly. Beneath the sequins, the dress felt like liquid silk. Flint had all he could do to stop his hands from caressing Francis instead of merely holding her firm so he could lift her off the horse.

"Where'd you get the horse, anyway?" Francis

forced her mind to start working. *Everything has a place,* she reminded herself. If she could only find the place of everything, this whole nightmare would come aright. She could make sense and order out of this whole madness if she worked at solving one piece of the puzzle and then went on to the next piece. She'd start with the horse.

"A small farm outside of Billings," Flint answered. His hands spanned Francis's rib cage. He could feel her heart pounding. "They rent horses."

"Why would you rent a horse?" Francis persisted. One question at a time. It helped her focus and forget about the hands around her. "You don't live around here. They must usually rent to ranchers."

Flint stopped. He could hardly say he needed a horse to rescue her. She'd never believe that. Then he remembered he didn't need an answer. "That's classified information. Government." Flint had her circled, and there was no reason to stall. "Move with me on the count of three."

All thought of the horse—and its order—fled Francis's mind.

"One. Two." Flint braced himself. "Three."

When Flint pulled, his hands slid from the middle of Francis's rib cage to the top. He almost stopped. But Honey was beginning to tap-dance around again, and he had to follow through.

Francis gasped. The man's hands were moving

upward from her rib cage. There was nothing for it but to put her arms around his neck and swing forward.

"Atta girl," Flint murmured. Even he didn't know if he was talking to Francis or the horse. And it didn't matter. He had Francis once again in his arms. Well, maybe not in his arms, but she was swinging from his neck. That had to count for something.

Francis winced. Her leg was swinging off the horse along with the rest of her body, and her leg was protesting. But she gritted her teeth. "Let me down."

Flint went from ice to fire in a heartbeat. He'd been without a jacket after he gave it to Francis, and his chest was cold. But the minute Francis swung against him, his whole insides flamed. His jacket had only been draped over her, and now it fell back to her shoulders. He felt the cool smoothness of her bare arms wrapped around his neck and the swell of her breasts pressed against his shirt.

"I can't let you down." Flint ground the words out. "You can't walk through a snowdrift in those heels."

"I can walk barefoot."

"Not with that leg," Flint shifted Francis's weight so his neck didn't carry her. Instead, he had his arms around her properly this time. There were no bad guys here. He could carry her like a gentleman. "Besides, you'd get frostbite."

Francis didn't argue. She simply couldn't think of anything to say. She had been swiveled, swept up in his arms and now rested on Flint's shoulder with a view of his chin. This was not the way anything was supposed to go. She was supposed to be forgetting him. "You nicked your chin the night of the prom, too."

"Huh?"

"When you shaved—the night of the prom, you nicked your chin. Almost in the same place."

"I was nervous."

"Me, too."

"You didn't look nervous," Flint said softly. He had tied Honey to a branch and was carrying Francis out of the pine grove. "You were cool as a cucumber."

"I hadn't been able to eat all day."

"You were perfect," Flint said simply. He was walking toward the small wood frame house. "Everybody is hungry at those things, anyway. You think there'll be food and it turns out to be pickled mushrooms or something with toothpicks in it."

Flint stopped. He was halfway to the house, and he knew someone had been here recently besides himself and Honey. A faint smell was coming from the house—the smell of cigars. He'd only known one man to ever smoke that particular brand.

"I'm going to set you down and check out the house," Flint whispered. It could be a trap. The cigars weren't a secret. "Be quiet."

Francis shivered, and not from the cold. Even in a whisper, Flint's voice sounded deadly serious. For the first time, she was truly afraid. And, for the first time, it occurred to her that if it were known by now that she was kidnapped—and it surely would be known once Jess checked around the barn—then someone would be out to rescue her. And if they intended to rescue her, they would also be out to hurt—maybe even kill—Flint.

The very thought of it turned her to ice. She could cheerfully strangle Flint herself. But seeing him hurt—really hurt—was something else again.

Think, Francis, think, she told herself as Flint slid her out of his arms to a dry space near a pine tree. The shade of the tree made the night darker here than anywhere. Even the light of the moon did not reflect off her sequins when she was sitting here. She could no longer see his face. He was a black shadow who crouched beside her.

"Be careful," she whispered at his back as he turned to leave. The words sounded futile to her ears. And then she saw his black silhouette as he drew a gun from somewhere. He must have had a gun in the saddlebag. Or maybe he had a shoulder holster.

Francis didn't want to be responsible for Flint being hurt. But anyone who was here to rescue her would think nothing of shooting Flint. *Think, Francis, think.* There had to be a solution. She couldn't just sit here and wait for the gunfire to begin.

That's it, she thought victoriously. She knew she could think of a solution. It just needed an orderly mind. If there were no kidnapping, there would be no need for any shooting.

Francis forced herself to stand. Her one leg wobbled, but it would have to do. She took a step forward, praying whoever was inside that wooden house would have sense enough to recognize her voice.

"Flint, darling," she called in what she hoped was a gay and flirtatious voice. She was out of practice, but even if her voice wasn't seductive she knew it was loud enough to be heard through the thickest walls. "I thought you said there was a bed inside this old house for us to use."

There, she thought in satisfaction, *that should quell any questions about a kidnapping.* It would, of course, raise all sorts of other questions, but she could deal with that later. She wondered who of the many Dry Creek men had come to her rescue.

Flint froze. Only years of training stopped him from turning around to stare at Francis. The deep easy chuckle that rumbled through the walls of the house confirmed his suspicions about who had smoked the cigars. The cigars could be duplicated. The chuckle never. It was safe to turn around.

Flint could only see the silhouette of Francis, but it was enough. He walked toward her and said the only thing he could think to say. "I told you to keep quiet. That could have been anyone inside."

"I didn't want you to be shot on my account," Francis whispered airily as she limped toward him. "If you just let me go now, there'll be no kidnapping."

"There never was a kidnapping. This was a rescue."

"A rescue?" Francis turned the word over in her mouth and spoke low enough so that whoever was inside the house could not hear. "Don't you think that's going a bit far? I don't think anyone would believe it's a rescue— I think we better stick with the seduction story."

Flint shook his head. No wonder being a hero was so difficult these days.

"Not that they'll believe the seduction story, either." Francis continued to whisper. Her leg was painful, but she found it easier to limp than to stand. "I must look a sight by now."

The deep darkness of the night that had gathered around the pine trees lifted as Francis moved toward him. "I wonder which of the men from Dry Creek knew enough to drive out here and wait for us. Pretty quick thinking."

Flint held his breath. In the night, he could look at Francis and not worry about the naked desire she would see in his eyes any other time. His jacket had fallen off her shoulders under the tree, and her arms and neck gleamed white even in the midnight darkness. The sequins of that red dress glittered as she moved, showing every curve in her slender body. She was beautiful.

"It's not one of the men from Dry Creek," Flint said softly. "It's my boss."

Francis stopped. She'd never thought—never even considered. And she should have—there's an order to everything, she reminded herself blindly. One needed to know the place of everything. And a kidnapping, she noted dully, required a motive and, in this case, a boss.

Francis stared unmoving at the weatherbeaten deserted house that used to belong to Flint's grandmother. The white paint had peeled off the frame years ago, leaving a chipped grayness that blended into the darkness. Gaping black holes marked where the glass had broken out of the windows.

"He must think I'm a fool," Francis whispered stiffly.

Francis looked so fragile, Flint moved slowly toward her. She looked like a bird, perched for flight even with her sprained leg muscle.

"No, I'm sure he doesn't think that at all," he said softly.

When he reached Francis, Flint picked her up again. This time he cradled her in his arms properly, as he had wanted to each time he'd picked her up tonight. For the first time, she didn't resist him. That should thrill his heart, Flint thought. But it didn't. He knew Francis wasn't warming toward him. She'd just given up.

"And that bit about the bed." Francis continued to fret. "I'm a middle-aged woman. He must think I'm a featherbrain—especially because he knows why you have me out here."

"He does, does he?" Flint asked quietly. It came as somewhat of a surprise to him that he'd rather have Francis kicking his shin with her pointed high heels than to have her lying still in his arms feeling foolish after having done something so brave.

The angle wasn't perfect for what he needed to do, but Flint found that if he bent his knee and slowly lowered Francis until she was securely perched on the knee, he could crane his neck and do what he needed to do.

He bent his head down and kissed her. He knew his lips were cold and chapped by now. He knew that the quick indrawn breath he heard from Francis was shock rather than passion. But he also knew that they both needed this kiss more than they needed the air they were breathing.

Flint took his time. He'd waited twenty years for this kiss and, planned or not, he needed to take his time. He felt the stiffness leave Francis's lips and he felt them move against him like they used to. He and his Francis were home again.

"Thank you." Francis was the first one to breathe after the kiss ended. Her pulse was beating fast, but she willed it to slow. "At least now your boss won't think I'm delusional—he'll think you at least tried to seduce me. Middle-aged or not." Francis stopped speaking to peer into the darkness of the broken windows. "He is watching, isn't he?"

For the first time since he'd bent down on one knee, Flint felt the bone-chilling cold of the snow beneath him. He might be home again, but Francis wasn't. "You think the kiss was for my boss's benefit?"

"Of course. And I appreciate it. I really do."

Flint only grunted. He must be losing his touch. He went back and picked up his jacket to wrap around Francis.

Chapter Three

"There's trouble in Dry Creek." The words came out of the other man's mouth the moment Flint kicked open the door to the abandoned house and, still holding Francis, stepped inside. "Kidnapping."

"I know," Francis said stiffly. She was glad she'd have the chance to show she wasn't a ninny. "That's me."

"Not unless you got here in the back of a cattle truck, it's not," the other man said mildly, a lit cigar in his mouth and a cell phone in his hand. The only light in the room was a small flashlight the man must have laid on the table recently. The flashlight gave a glow to the rather large room and showed some bookcases and a few wooden chairs scattered around the table.

"Well, surely there's no point in kidnapping more than me."

"It appears they have some woman named Sylvia Bannister and then Garth Elkton."

"Oh, no." Francis half twisted herself out of Flint's arms. "I'll need to go help them."

"You can't go." Flint finished carrying her over to one of the chairs and gently sat her down.

"That's right. I'm a prisoner."

"You're not a prisoner," Flint said impatiently and then turned to the older man. "It better be me that goes. I've gotten a little acquainted with the guys responsible for this. Might have picked up a tip or two."

While Flint was talking, he was rummaging through a backpack resting on another chair. He pulled out an ammunitions cartridge and put it in the pocket of a dry jacket that was wrapped around the back of the chair. Then he pulled out a pair of leather gloves.

"Mrs. B called it in." The older man gestured to his cell phone. "Said to hurry. Some kids are chasing the truck in a bus as we speak. You can use my Jeep. Parked it behind the trees over there." The older man jerked his head in the opposite direction they had ridden in from. "It'll get you there faster."

"Not faster than Honey," Flint said with a smile as he walked toward the door. "She can beat a Jeep any day. She makes her own roads."

Flint opened the door and was gone in a little less than five seconds. Francis knew it was five seconds because she was counting to ten and had only reached five when the door creaked shut. Her teeth were chattering and she didn't know if it was because she was near frozen or because she was scared to death. She hoped counting would force her to focus and make it all better. It didn't.

"I've got one of those emergency blankets in here someplace," the older man said as he turned to a backpack of his own leaning in the corner of the room. "Prevents heat loss, that sort of thing."

"I'm okay." Francis shivered through the words. She felt helpless to be sitting here when someone had kidnapped Sylvia and Garth.

"Not much to that dress," the older man said as he walked over to her and wrapped what looked like a huge foil paper around her. "Especially in ten below weather."

The paper crinkled when she moved, but Francis noticed a pocket of warmth was forming around her legs. It would spread. "I didn't plan to be out in it for so long without my coat."

"I expect you didn't." The man went back to his pack and pulled out a small hand-cranked lantern. He twisted the handle a few times and set the lantern on the table. A soft glow lit up the whole room. "Something must have gone wrong."

"Flint kidnapped me."

That fact seemed to amuse the older man. "Yes, I forgot. You mentioned that earlier. Sorry to spoil your plans."

"They were hardly my plans. You're the boss. They were your plans." Francis knew it wasn't always wise to confront criminals. But the old man seemed fairly harmless, and she did like to keep things clear.

"Sounded more like a lover's tryst to me." The man sat on one of the chairs.

"Humph." Francis didn't want to go into that.

"Not that it's any of my business," the man continued and looked around the room. "Although I can assure you that if Flint told you there was a bed, he lied."

"Humph." Francis was feeling the warmth steel up her whole body. She could almost feel cozy. "We don't really need a bed."

"Good."

The man sat for a few minutes in silence and then got up and went to his pack and drew out a can. "Peaches?"

"I'd like that."

The man opened the peaches with the can-opening edge of a Swiss knife.

"Handy thing," he said as he flipped the blades into the knife and put it in his pocket. "Flint gave me this one almost fifteen years ago now."

"You've known him for that long?"

The man nodded. "Almost as long as you have if you're who I think you are."

Francis wondered if this were a trick to find out who she was. But then, she reasoned, it hardly mattered. Flint certainly knew who she was, and he would be back soon to tell his boss anyway.

"I'm Francis Elkton."

The man nodded again. "Thought you must be. But I guess I'll share my peaches with you anyway. Figure you must have had your reasons for what you did."

"Reasons for what?"

The man shrugged. "It's old history. Flint went on and so did you. I wouldn't even have remembered your full name if I hadn't seen that."

There it was. The man was pointing to a faded family Bible. One of those with the black leather cover stamped, Our Family With God.

"I'm in there?" Francis moved outside the warmth of the foil blanket to stand up and walk to the bookcase. The Bible was closed, but she saw that a ribbon marker had been left through the center of the book. Curious, she opened it.

The man was right. There was her name. Francis Elkton.

The words read, "United in Holy Matrimony Flint L. Harris and Francis Elkton on the day of our Lord, April 17—"

"Who wrote that there?" Even the temperature

outside could not match the ice inside her. She'd never seen the words like that, so black and white.

The man shrugged. "It was either Flint or his grandmother."

"His grandmother didn't know we—" Francis gulped. She could hardly say they had gotten married when the most they had done was perform a mock ceremony.

"Then it must have been Flint."

"He must have stopped here before he left that day."

The man nodded. "I expect so. A man like Flint takes his marriage vows serious. He'd want to at least write them down in a family Bible."

"There were no marriage vows," Francis corrected the man bitterly. "We said them before a fake justice of the peace."

The man looked startled. "There was nothing fake about your vows."

Francis felt a headache start in the back of her neck. "I'm afraid there was. The justice of the peace was a phony."

"I checked him out. He was pure gold."

"You can't have checked him out. He didn't even exist. Phony name and everything."

Francis still remembered the smug look on her father's face when he got off the phone with a city official in Las Vegas and informed her there was no such justice of the peace.

The peaches were forgotten. The older man looked cautiously at Francis and said softly, "I did a thorough check on Flint myself before he came into the Bureau. I knew he had potential and would go far. I wanted to be sure we did a complete check. I talked to the justice of the peace personally. And the county sheriff who arrested Flint on that speeding ticket."

Francis felt her headache worsen. "What speeding ticket?"

The old man looked at Francis silently for a moment. "The day after you were married, Flint was arrested on a speeding ticket just inside the Miles City limits. Thirty-eight in a thirty-five-mile-an-hour zone."

"No one gets a ticket for that."

"Flint did. And because he didn't have the hundred thousand dollars cash to post bail, he did ninety days in jail."

Francis put her hand to her head. "That can't be. No one does that kind of time on a traffic ticket— and they certainly don't have that kind of bail."

The man kept looking at Francis like he was measuring her. Then he continued slowly. "I talked to the sheriff who made the arrest. He was doing a favor for someone. The arrest. The high bail. The ninety days. It was all a personal favor."

"Flint never hurt anyone. Who would do that?"

The silence was longer this time. Finally, the man

spoke. "The sheriff said it was you. Said you'd changed your mind about the marriage and didn't have the nerve to tell Flint to his face."

"Me?" The squeak that came out of Francis's throat was one she scarcely recognized as her own.

The man looked away to give her privacy. "Not that it's really any of my business."

Francis needed to breathe. *Reason this out,* she said to herself. *Reason it out. Put the pieces in their places. It will make sense. There's an order to it all. You just need to find it.*

"But I hadn't changed my mind." Francis grabbed hold of that one fact and hung on to it. The whole story revolved around that one piece, and that one piece was false. That must make the whole story false. "I wanted to be married to Flint."

The man lifted his eyes to look at her. With the soft light of the lantern on the table, Francis could see the pity in the man's eyes. "I'm beginning to think that might possibly be true."

Francis was numb. She'd fallen into a gaping hole and she didn't know how to get out of it. She couldn't talk. She could barely think. "But who would do such a thing?"

Francis knew it was her father. Knew it in her heart before she had reasoned it out with her head. He was the only one who could have done it.

Her father had been upset when she and Flint had driven up and announced their marriage. She hadn't expected her father to be glad about the marriage, but she thought he'd adjust in time. She'd been relieved when Flint had suggested he drive into Miles City to buy roses for her. If she had some time alone with her father, Francis had thought, she could change his mind.

She and her father had talked for a while and then she went in to pack. There wasn't much she needed to take. Some tea towels she'd made years ago when her mother was alive to help her. The clothes she'd been wearing to school. A few pieces of costume jewelry. The letters Garth had written her when he was overseas.

She'd filled up two suitcases when her father came in to say he'd called Las Vegas and found out that the justice of the peace was a fake.

At that moment, Francis had not worried about her father's words. If the justice of the peace was a fake, she'd calmly reasoned, she and Flint would only find someone else to marry them again. Flint had made a mistake in locating the proper official, but they would take care of it. They'd marry again. That's what people in love did. She started to fold the aprons her mother had given her.

When she finished packing, Francis went down to the kitchen to prepare supper for her father. It was the last meal she'd make for him for awhile, and she was happy to do it. She decided to make beef stew because it could simmer for hours with little tending after she left.

Four hours later her father invited her to sit down and eat the stew with him. She knew Flint could have driven into Miles City and back several times in the hours that had passed. Francis refused the stew and went to her room. He must have had car trouble, she thought. That was it. He'd call any minute. She stayed awake all night waiting for the phone to ring. It was a week before she even made any attempt to sleep at nights.

"It was my father," Francis said calmly as she looked Flint's boss in the eyes. "He must have arranged it all."

"I'm sorry." The man said his words quickly.

The inside of the cold house was silent. Francis sat with the open Bible on her lap, staring at the page where her marriage vows had been recorded and a scripture reference from Solomon had been added. As she looked at it closely, she could see that the faded handwriting was Flint's. She wished she could have stood with him when he recorded the date in this Bible. It must have had meaning for him or he wouldn't have stopped on his way into Miles City to write it down.

"Surely Flint—" she looked at the man.

He was twisting the handle that gave energy to the emergency lantern on the table. He didn't look up from the lantern. "He didn't want to tell me about you. Didn't even mention your name. But he had to tell me the basics. I was only checking out his story. Part of the job. We needed to find out about the arrest. It was on his record.''

"So he thinks it was me who got him arrested.''

The temperature of the night seemed to go even lower.

The man nodded.

Francis felt numb. She had never imagined anything like this. She had assumed Flint had been the one to have second thoughts. Or that he had never intended to really marry her anyway. He wasn't from around here. She never should have trusted him as much as she did. She repeated all the words she had said to herself over the years. None of them gave her any comfort.

"He should have come back to talk to me.''

"Maybe he tried,'' the man said. He'd stopped cranking the lantern and sat at the table.

The silence stretched between them.

"Mind if I smoke?'' the man finally asked.

"Go ahead,'' Francis said automatically. She felt like her whole life was shifting gears and the gears were rusty. She'd spent too much of the past twenty years resenting Flint. Letting her anger burn toward him in the hopes that someday her memories would be light, airy ashes that could be blown away. But instead of producing ashes that were light, her anger had produced a heavy, molten chunk of resentment that wouldn't budge in a whirlwind.

There had been no blowing away of old, forgotten memories. These past weeks in Dry Creek had already proven that to her. She was beginning to believe she would be forever shackled by her memories. But now it turned out that the whole basis for her anger was untrue. Flint had not left her. She had, apparently, somehow left him.

A rumbling growl came from the man's coat pocket.

"Excuse me," he said as he reached into his pocket and pulled out a cell phone. "That'll be Mrs. B."

The conversation was short, and all Francis heard were several satisfied grunts.

"Flint's got them in custody," the man said when he put his phone back in his pocket. "He's holding them in something he called the dance barn in Dry Creek. Said you'd know where it was. Told me to bring you with me and come over."

"So I'm free to go?" Francis asked blankly as she looked up. She'd been so distressed about everything the man had told her she hadn't realized her first impressions of him must not be true.

"Of course," the man said as he stood and put his backpack on his shoulders.

"But who are you?"

"Inspector Kahn—FBI," the man said as he fumbled through another pocket in his coat and pulled out an identification badge.

"But—"

"The cattle business," the man explained as he showed the badge to Francis. "It's interstate. Makes it a federal crime."

"So the FBI sent someone in." Francis took a moment to look at the badge so she could scramble to get on track. She had heard the FBI was working on the case. They had asked Garth to help. "So you really didn't need Garth, after all."

Inspector Kahn grunted. "Not when I have a hothead like Flint working for me."

"Flint works for you?"

Inspector Kahn grunted again and started walking toward the door. "Sometimes I think it's me working for him. I'd place money that the reason he's so keen for me to get there is because he wants me to do the paperwork. Flint always hated the paper side of things." He looked over his shoulder at her. "You coming?"

"Yes." Francis certainly didn't want to stay in this cold house any longer than she needed to. She pulled the jacket Flint had given her earlier over her shoulders and picked up the Bible.

The inspector looked at the Bible. "I expect you'll need to talk to Flint about this marriage business."

"I intend to try."

The inspector smiled at that. "Flint isn't always an easy man to reason with. Stubborn as he is brave. But you know that—you're married to him."

"I guess I am, at that." The ashes inside of Francis might not be blowing away, but she could feel them shifting all over the place. It appeared she, Francis K. Elkton, had actually been married to Flint L. Harris some twenty years ago.

For the umpteenth time that night, Flint wondered at the value of being a hero. He had saved Garth Elkton's hide—not to mention the even more tender hide of the attractive woman with him, Sylvia Bannister—and they were both giving him a shoulder colder than the storm front that was fast moving into town.

In his jeans and wool jacket, Flint was out of place inside the barn. Not that any of the men there hadn't quickly helped him hog-tie the three men who had kidnapped Garth and Sylvia and attempted to take them away in the back of an old cattle truck.

But the music was still playing a slow tune and the pink crepe paper still hung from the rafters of that old barn. And Flint felt about as welcome as a stray wet dog at a fancy church picnic.

"There, that should do it." Flint checked the knots in the rope for the third time. He'd asked someone to call the local sheriff and was told the man was picking up something in Billings but would be back at the dance soon. He hoped the sheriff would get there before the inspector. Maybe then some of the paperwork would be local.

"Who'd you say you were again?" Garth Elkton asked the question, quiet-like, as he squatted to check the ropes with Flint.

"Flint Harris."

"The guy who called me the other night about the kidnapping?" Garth sounded suspicious.

"Yes."

"Still don't know how you knew about it."

"Because I've been freezing my toes off the past few nights following these guys around." Flint jerked his head at the men on the floor. Flint could see the direction Garth was going with his questions and he didn't appreciate it. "If I was one of them, don't you think they'd at least recognize me?"

Flint looked at the three men on the floor. They looked quarrelsome and pathetic. He didn't appreciate being lumped in with them. But at least it was clear that none of them claimed to have ever seen him before now.

"They didn't seem too clear about who their boss was," Garth continued mildly. "Could be they wouldn't recognize the man."

"I can't tell you who their boss is, but he's using a local informant," Flint said in exasperation. "We've got that much figured out. And I'm not local."

"You were local enough for my sister."

Ah, so it's come to that, Flint thought. It seemed he'd never get a square break from an Elkton. "Let's leave your sister out of it."

The mention of his sister made Garth scan the room. "Where is she, anyway? Thought she'd be back inside by now. I heard Jess was looking for her."

"She was with me." Flint resigned himself to his fate.

"With you? What was she doing with you?"

"Don't worry. She'll be back here any minute now."

"She better be or—" Garth seemed unaware that his voice was rising.

"Now, now, boys."

Flint looked up. He'd recognize that voice anywhere. He grinned as he looked at the woman who had been his grandmother's staunch friend in her final days. "Mrs. Hargrove! How are you?"

Mrs. Hargrove had aged a little in the years since he'd seen her last. And she was wearing a long velvet maroon dress tonight instead of her usual cotton gingham housedress. But she held herself with the same innate dignity he always expected from her. "Doing just fine, thank you."

"You know him?" Garth asked Mrs. Hargrove skeptically.

"Of course," the woman replied warmly. "He

was in my Sunday school class for six months when he was here, and if he doesn't get up off that floor and give me a hug pretty soon, I'm going to be mighty disappointed.''

Flint felt less like an unwelcome dog just looking at the woman. He stood up and enfolded her in his arms.

"I still miss that grandmother of yours," Mrs. Hargrove whispered as she held him.

"So do I," he whispered back.

"It comforts me to know she's with our Lord," she added and then leaned back to look Flint in the eye. "And I'm still working on her final request of me."

"Oh?" This was something Flint had not heard about.

"I pray for you every day, son," Mrs. Hargrove said with satisfaction. "Just like she would be doing if she were alive."

Flint had faced bullets. But nothing had made him feel as vulnerable as those words did. In his astonishment, he mumbled the only thing he could think of. "Well, thank you." To his further amazement, he meant it.

"And here you've come back to us a hero." Mrs. Hargrove stepped out of his arms and spoke loudly so that everyone could hear. "This is Essie Harris's grandson, folks. Let's give him a good welcome home."

With those words, Flint was transformed from the unwelcome stray into the prize guest. A murmur of approval ran through the folks of Dry Creek, and he heard more than one person mutter that it was about time.

"Here, let me introduce you around," Mrs. Hargrove said as she took Flint's arm. "You probably don't remember everyone. Here, this is Doris June—you might have met her, she went to school with Francis."

Flint found himself shaking hands with an attractive blond woman about his age. "You were a cheerleader, weren't you?"

The woman nodded. "The coach was always hoping to find a way to get you to try out for the basketball team."

"I was busy helping my grandmother."

"I know." The blonde smiled.

"And this is Margaret Ann." Mrs. Hargrove moved him on to another pleasant woman.

Flint noticed Mrs. Hargrove introduced him to the women first. The men hung back. They didn't seem as willing to shake his hand as the women were. In fact, some of them still looked at him with suspicion thick on their faces.

"Francis should be here soon," he said to no one in particular. He knew why the men didn't trust him. "She really is fine."

Flint had no sooner finished his words of reassurance than the barn door opened and his words came true. Francis was back.

The men of Dry Creek looked at Francis in disbelief and then looked at Flint, the suspicion hardening on their faces.

Flint would have cursed if Mrs. Hargrove wasn't standing, speechless, at his elbow.

Francis stood inside the doorway. She must have had dropped the jacket on her way inside, because she wasn't wearing it, and her neck and arms were pearl white. Her hair tumbled around her head in a mass of black silk that was sprinkled with dry pine needles. She had a bruise on her arm that was deepening into a ripe purple.

Flint could have tried to explain away the bruise and the needles. But he knew he'd have a more difficult time talking his way past the ragged tear in Francis's dress that went from her ankles to a few inches short of her waist. Even now Francis had to hold her dress shut around her with one hand while she carried something behind her back in the other hand.

"It was the horse," Flint stammered into the silence. He'd been called to testify in federal drug investigations, but he'd never felt the pressure of his testimony like now.

"She was with you." The quiet steel in Garth's voice came from behind him and prodded. "What happened?"

"Now, boys." Mrs. Hargrove found her breath and interrupted again. "Can't you see Francis is frozen to the bone? There'll be time for sorting this all out later."

Flint met the metal in Garth's eyes and smiled inside. He might not like the steel at his back, but he was warmed to know that Francis had such a loyal protector.

"Nothing," Flint assured the other man quietly. "Francis is fine."

Chapter Four

Francis blinked. Her eyes had become accustomed to the black night, and when she stepped into the golden light inside the barn, she felt like a spotlight was on her. She blinked again before she realized that every single person in the barn, even those three men tied in a muddle at Garth's feet, were staring at her.

"What happened to the music?" Francis took an uncertain step forward. The audio system that someone had set up was attached to an old record player, and the scratchy music it had been playing was reminiscent of the fifties. Before she'd gone to look for the Big Dipper an hour or so ago, however, the record hadn't skipped like the one that was on in the background now. "Why isn't anyone dancing?"

"Are you all right, dear?" Mrs. Hargrove was the first to move, and she stepped toward Francis.

"I'm fine—fine," Francis stammered. She looked at her dress, and for the first time realized how she must look. The fabric on her ill-fated red dress was thin in the best of circumstances, but the section she held in her hand was nothing more than fly away threads held together by sequins. "It was the horse."

"The horse did that to your dress?" Garth asked, disbelieving, as he, too, stepped forward.

"Well, no, I ripped the dress when I tried to get off the horse." Francis realized as she said the words that they didn't sound very plausible. The polite eyes of her neighbors told her they didn't believe her. She tried again, a little defensively. "Well, I wasn't just getting off—I was going to ride Honey so I needed to swing my leg around."

"It doesn't matter, dear," Mrs. Hargrove said soothingly as she patted Francis on the shoulder, and then exclaimed, "Why you're ice cold! Come over by the heaters."

Tall electric heaters stood at the far side of the barn. Garth had them installed when the barn was used several months ago for the Christmas pageant. Francis let Mrs. Hargrove start leading her over to them.

"Here, let me carry that for you," Mrs. Hargrove offered as she held out her hand.

"Oh, it's nothing," Francis said quickly. She let go of the threads of her dress so she could slip Flint's family Bible under her arm more securely. She didn't know how Flint would feel about her taking the Bible, even though he'd left it in his grandmother's deserted house years ago and any stranger traveling through could have picked it up and taken it. That fact had bothered her the whole ride in. How could he leave something like that— something that spoke of their wedding—for strangers to take? Or for the wind to blow away?

Sequins fell from her dress as she hobbled closer to the heat. She felt a long shaft of cold on her leg where her dress was torn and a small circle of even colder metal where her garter fastened to her nylons.

A ripple of slow, approving murmurs moved through the group of men—most of them single ranch hands—already standing near the heaters.

Flint felt every muscle in his body tense. He didn't know which of those men around the heaters was Francis's boyfriend, but Flint didn't think much of him. What kind of man would let other men see that much leg of his girlfriend? Especially when the girlfriend looked like Francis. He doubted there was an unmarried man here tonight who wouldn't go to bed with the image of those red threads trailing across Francis's leg.

"Doesn't anybody use tablecloths anymore?"

Flint took a dozen long strides to get to the food table and looked around impatiently. The tables were wrapped in a pink bridal paper with pink streamers placed every few inches twisting from the table to the floor.

"You're hungry?" Francis stopped to stare at Flint.

Flint only grunted as he tore several of the streamers from the back of the table. "These will have to do."

The streamers were wide, and Flint had his hand full of them when he kneeled by Francis. "Hold still."

Flint began wrapping the streamers around Francis, starting at her waist and moving on to her hips. The crepe paper wasn't any heavier than the material in that red sequin dress, but it held the pieces of Francis's dress together. Flint knotted the first strip around her waist as an anchor and then began to wrap her like a mummy from her waist to her knees.

"I can do it," Francis said as she shifted awkwardly to keep the book behind her back.

If Francis hadn't acted so uncomfortable, Flint would have taken at least another minute before he focused on the book she was obviously trying to hide from him.

"That's Grandma's," Flint said, tight-lipped. He supposed Francis had read what he wrote that day.

Well, there was nothing for it. He had been a fool, but he wouldn't apologize.

He remembered the day he'd arrived at his grandmother's house after leaving Francis at her father's to pack. His grandmother had been at a church meeting in Dry Creek and wasn't home. On impulse Flint had pulled his grandmother's family Bible off the shelf and recorded his marriage. Then he put the Bible back.

The book wasn't his grandmother's reading Bible, but it was important to her nonetheless. Her wedding and the wedding of Flint's parents had been recorded on its center pages. He planned to pull the Bible out and surprise his grandmother when he came back from Miles City that day.

But it was three months before he came back from Miles City, and by then the ink would have been fully dried on the divorce papers he'd signed in jail. He had no calm words to explain what had happened, so he left the Bible on the shelf. As angry as he was with Francis, he didn't want the good people of Dry Creek to force her into accepting a marriage she didn't want. He didn't even tell his grandmother what had happened. If she ever saw the words, she never asked about them in their weekly phone conversations.

Even after all these years, Flint still didn't want Francis to be publicly blamed. He doubted the good people of Dry Creek would think much of a woman who abandoned her marriage vows within hours of saying them. They might not be as forgiving as he had learned to be.

"Don't worry. Your secret's safe," Flint murmured as he impatiently knotted one of the crepe streamers just above Francis's knee. He wished there was more noise in this old barn, but it seemed like everyone would rather watch him wrap Francis in crepe paper than dance with each other. "You were just a kid. I'm the one who should have had sense enough to stop it before it went as far as it did."

"I was no more a kid than you were. I was certainly old enough to know my own mind," Francis snapped back in a low whisper. She hadn't counted on having this conversation in front of a hundred curious witnesses with Flint kneeling in front of her and angrily wrapping crepe paper around her legs. But if that was the only way to have it, she'd do it. "You should have realized that instead of—"

"Me?" Flint reared back when he finally heard the mild tone of reproof in Francis's voice. It was one thing to forgive her. But it was asking a bit much of him to let her take that tone with him. "I should have realized something? The only thing I should have realized was that you were too young for the responsibilities involved in getting mar—"

Flint suddenly heard the silence. The bride and groom who were celebrating their wedding tonight were standing still as statues. Even the men tied together into a pile at Garth's feet had stopped scraping their feet along the wood floor. A hundred people were watching, and no one was crumpling a paper cup or moving in their chair. Someone had shut off the record player, so even that empty scratching had stilled. This old barn had never been so quiet.

Flint willed his voice to a mild whisper. "You were a bit young, is all. That's not a crime."

"It would have been a crime if I hadn't been so caught up in my career," Francis replied as the reality of the situation became a little clearer. Bigamy. What if she had married, never knowing that she was already married? She wondered if the law forgave such silliness. "You at least knew we were married."

"Married?" The word was picked up by someone standing near them and passed around the barn quicker than a fake dollar bill at a carnival.

Flint looked up as a new group of men slowly gathered from around the barn and moved over by the heaters. These men had a look about them he'd seen in combat. He'd wager the lot of them worked for Francis's brother. They all had calluses on their hands and scuffed boots on their feet. He expected he could take any of them in a fair fight. By the hardening looks on their faces, he figured he'd have to do that very thing before the night was over.

"Maybe we better discuss this outside," Flint

said calmly as he stood up, twisted the last piece of crepe paper into a tidy roll and set it on the corner of the refreshment table.

Flint didn't want to call Francis a liar in front of her family and friends, but if she thought he'd buy some story about her being drunk or confused that night in Vegas, she was going to be disappointed. He knew she hadn't had a drop of liquor to drink. They hadn't even opened the complimentary champagne that came with the wedding ceremony. And, while she had been wonderfully starry-eyed, she had not been confused.

Francis nodded. The warmth from the heaters was uneven, and she shivered. "Let me look for my jacket."

Francis ran her eyes over the people in the barn, looking for Sylvia Bannister. The last time she'd seen Sylvia she had been wearing Francis's black lion jacket, a remembrance from long-ago high school years. As Francis looked over the small clusters of her friends and neighbors, they began to shuffle in sudden embarrassment and start to move.

"You're welcome to borrow my jacket." Mrs. Hargrove stepped forward efficiently with a wool jacket in her hands. "I won't be needing it since I'll be dancing—if someone will put the music back on."

The crowd took the hint. Someone flipped a switch, and an old Beatles song started to play. A few of the women walked to the refreshment table and poured more punch in the bowl. The kidnappers, tied in a heap to one side of the barn, started to twist their rope-bound feet and complain that there wasn't even a local law official there to see to their comfort.

"We got our rights, too," the stocky brother started to protest. "Ain't right we're kept tied up like this just so he—" the man jerked his head at Flint "—can play Romeo in some snowdrift with his Juliet."

"Yeah." One of the other brothers took his lead. "We ain't even had supper."

"I'm not feeding you supper," Flint said in clipped exasperation, although he almost welcomed the excuse to turn from Francis and focus on business for a minute. "Give me a break, you've only been arrested for fifteen minutes. And it's almost midnight—you should have eaten supper hours ago."

"Well, we didn't get a chance to eat before." The brother whined.

"You should always take time for a proper meal," Francis said automatically as she slipped her arms into the jacket Mrs. Hargrove held out for her. "Good nutrition makes for a more productive worker."

Flint snorted as he nodded his head toward the kidnappers. "Trust me, they don't need to be more productive."

"I think there's some of those little quiche appetizers left," Mrs. Hargrove said as she headed for the refreshment table. "The Good Book says we need to look out for our enemies."

"The Good Book says a lot of things," Flint said as his eyes skimmed over Francis. Yes, she still had it in her hand. His grandmother's Bible. "Not all of the things written in its pages are true."

Flint heard Mrs. Hargrove gasp, and he hurried to explain. "I mean some of the things that are handwritten—by a person in their own Bible—aren't necessarily true."

"Essie stood by everything she wrote in that Bible of hers." Mrs. Hargrove defended her friend. "And I'd stand by them, too."

"It wasn't something Grandma wrote," Flint said softly. He suddenly had a picture of his grandmother sitting down in the evening at her old wooden table and reading her Bible. She'd have her apron on and the radio humming in the background as she'd mouth the words. She read silently, but occasionally—when the words seemed either too wonderful or too horrible to be held in—she'd speak them aloud to whomever stood by.

Flint had never seen anyone else read a book like it was a letter that had come in the morning mail. He had secretly envied her the faith she had even though he knew it wasn't for the likes of him. Even then he didn't feel like he'd ever clean up good enough to merit much faith. But his grandmother was a different story. He didn't want anyone to question his grandmother's faith. "It wasn't something she wrote down. It was something I wrote. By mistake."

Mrs. Hargrove looked Flint full in the eyes before she smiled. "I can't think of a better place to write something—whether it's a mistake or not, only God knows."

Flint snorted. "Well, God isn't the only one who knows on this one. Wish He was. At least He can keep a secret."

"I can keep a secret." Francis was stung.

"I'm not worried about you, sweetheart," Flint said wryly as he smiled at her. "It's my boss I'm worried about. I know you can keep this secret— you've kept it for the past twenty years."

"Sometimes a secret needs a good airing out," Mrs. Hargrove offered breezily as she finished stacking some petite quiches on a small paper plate and started toward the tangle of men on the floor. "Especially those old ones."

By now several couples were dancing, and those who weren't dancing had politely turned their attention to other things.

"We do need to talk about it," Francis said firmly as she pulled the wool jacket closer around her. She searched in the pocket and found a hairpin. Just what she needed. She swept her hair up and gave it a couple of twists. Organizing her hair into a neat bun made her feel more in control. "There are things you don't know."

Flint stood by helplessly and watched the transformation of Francis. She'd gone from being a bewitching damsel in distress with handfuls of silken hair to a very competent-looking executive who wouldn't tolerate a hair out of place or a thought that wasn't useful.

"You don't need to make it right with me, if that's what you're thinking." Flint didn't want to have this final conversation with Francis. He was quite sure the executive Francis didn't approve of that long-ago Francis who had run off to be married. "Whatever happened on that day to make you change your mind, it is okay. I've made my peace with it."

"But that's not the way it was at all," Francis protested.

Francis buttoned the wool jacket around her. Mrs. Hargrove was several sizes larger than she was, and Francis liked the secure feeling the too-large jacket gave her. She must look a sight with the green plaid jacket on top of her skirt of pink crepe paper and red sequins.

"Speaking of the inspector, where is he?" Flint knelt to test the knots on the three men sitting patiently on the floor. He looked at Francis briefly. "Thought he was coming with you."

"He was. He got a call from the sheriff saying he had a flat tire down the road a piece. The inspector went to help him."

Flint grunted as he finished checking the knots. "He just wants to avoid the paperwork with these guys."

The door opened, and a square of cold midnight was visible for a moment before the inspector stepped inside the old barn and brushed a few stray snowflakes off his coat. "Did I hear you say paperwork? Don't worry about that. I'll do it."

Flint had never heard the inspector volunteer to do the paperwork.

"You'll maybe want to…" The inspector had walked over to where Flint knelt and inclined his head slightly in the direction of Francis.

So much for privacy, Flint thought. But if he talked to Francis here, the inspector wouldn't be the only one listening. "I'll talk to her later."

"That's too late." The inspector leaned down and whispered, "You better do it now before—"

The door to the barn opened again, and the inspector groaned. "Too late. He's here."

Flint looked at the open doorway but didn't see what the problem was. It was only the sheriff. The man looked decidedly uncomfortable, with patches of snow stuck to his jeans and his parka pulled close around his head. Tonight wasn't the best night for getting a flat tire.

Then the sheriff stepped all the way inside, and Flint noticed two other people crowding in the door behind him.

They both had big city stamped all over them. The woman was tall, lean and platinum. Her face was pinched with cold, but that didn't take away the look of expensive makeup. Definitely uptown.

The man was more downtown. Flint would peg him as a banker. Maybe vice president or loans officer. He had the look of a bean counter, but not the look of command. He was wearing a brown business suit and lined leather gloves. Expensive gloves, Flint thought a little jealously, wondering what snowdrift his own gloves had ended up in tonight.

"Robert!" the woman exclaimed loudly and started walking to the man Flint knew to be Robert Buckwalter.

So that was it, Flint thought as he stood up quickly. The inspector must be worried that the woman would interfere with Mrs. Buckwalter's secret cover.

No one knew that Mrs. Buckwalter was working with the FBI on this rustling business, not even her son. Until they found out the identity of the person serving as the informant for the rustling outfit, they couldn't be too careful about strangers. Especially strangers who wanted to cozy up to FBI operatives and their families.

Ordinarily Flint wouldn't seriously suspect the

woman. Not because she looked flimsy, but because he was pretty sure the informant had to be someone local. Only a local would have a cover good enough to have escaped everyone's notice and still have access to the information the rustlers would need.

Flint intercepted the blonde's path just before she reached Robert. "I'll need to see some identification."

The woman momentarily flushed guiltily, and Flint looked at her more closely. She was up to something.

"Identification?" She stopped and schooled her face into blankness. "I don't need identification. I'm with him." She pointed to Robert.

Flint couldn't help noticing Robert flinching as the other man protested. "Now, Laurel, you know that's not—"

Flint almost felt sorry for the man. He'd seen Robert earlier, working as a kitchen helper to the young woman chef his mother had sent out here with a planeload of lobsters for the party tonight. Flint had seen Robert land his small plane near Garth's ranch a few days ago in the early morning hours. A man as rich as Robert—with the whole Buckwalter fortune at his feet—would have to be besotted to slice radishes for two hours. "She's with you?"

"I wouldn't say with." Robert stumbled. He glanced at the young woman standing next to him in apology. "I know Laurel—of course I know her—our families are—well, my mother knows her better, so, no—I wouldn't say with."

"It was with enough for you on Christmas!" Laurel staged a pout that would do justice to a Hollywood starlet.

"Well." Flint backed away. He would have liked to help Robert out—he seemed like a decent man—but the FBI couldn't arrest a woman for flirting.

It wasn't until Flint turned that he realized his tactical mistake. The inspector wasn't worried about the woman. He was worried about that man who was walking to Francis with a determined look in his eyes that demanded she welcome him.

"You must be the boyfriend," Flint said as he walked to Francis. It was inevitable. The evening had been doomed from the start.

"I hope I'm more than a boyfriend," the man said, a little smugly, Flint thought, as he reached Francis and leaned over to peck her on her lips. "Now that she's had time away to think about things."

"Sam." Francis marveled that her voice sounded calm. She felt a growing urge to scream. "What are you doing here?"

"Well, I got to thinking. It's time you came back—how much thinking can a woman do?" The man laughed a little too heartily. "So I flew up to get you."

"Now's not a good time."

"Oh, I know. The inspector was telling me there's been lots of excitement here tonight. Seemed to think I'd be better off going back to Billings for the night, but I told him it was nonsense. It would take more than a few bad guys to rattle my Francis. She's the most sensible woman I've ever known."

Flint thought the man must be blind to think "sensible" summed up a woman like Francis. Didn't he see the shy warmth in her eyes when she first met someone? Hadn't he felt the slight tremble of her lips when she was kissed?

"Known a lot of women, have you?" Flint asked the man. He refused to think of the man as Sam. As far as Flint was concerned, the man had no name. And no future.

"Huh?"

Flint admitted the man didn't look like he could have known many women, but that didn't stop Flint from resenting him. "Just checking up on your background."

"Flint's with the FBI," Francis said, tight-lipped with annoyance. "He checks up on everybody."

"Oh, well, that's okay then." The man smiled at Flint and held out his hand. "Always nice to meet one of our nation's security men. Men like you keep us all safe."

Flint grunted. The man made it sound like Flint was a school crossing guard. Important enough for someone who did that sort of thing. Flint wondered if Francis actually loved the guy. He glared at the man until the man dropped his hand.

"You own a house?" Flint knew women loved big houses.

"A bedroom loft condo in downtown Denver," the man said with pride. "The Executive Manor complex."

Flint grunted. Close enough. The only house he could claim as his own was sitting just north of here on five desolate acres only chickens could love.

"Francis would want a tree or two."

The man looked startled. "I told her we could get a few ficus plants. They'd do."

Flint nodded. Francis just might settle for them, after all. Suddenly, Flint felt old. He had lived too hard and fast. At least the man standing before him looked stable. Maybe that was enough.

"You ever kill a man?"

"I beg your pardon?" The man was looking at Flint in alarm.

"It's a simple question—ever been in the military?"

The man shook his head. "Bad feet."

"Ever been arrested?"

"Of course not." The man was indignant. "And I certainly don't see the point of these questions— if I'm under suspicion for something I have a right to know. And if you're planning to arrest me, I demand a chance to call my attorney.''

Flint smiled wryly. He almost wished he could arrest the man. ''No, I'm just checking up on you.''

''Well, I'll let it go this time,'' the man said pompously. ''Mostly because the inspector here said you'd rescued Francis from those hoodlums. I should be thanking you for helping my fiancée, not sitting here arguing.''

''Fiancée.'' Flint felt a cold draft down his neck. It appeared the ficus had won.

''I never agreed to marry you.'' Francis felt the need to sit down and start counting. Everything was unraveling. ''Actually, I can't marry you.''

''Nonsense. Of course you can. I've thought about it, too, you know. Granted, we don't have some fairy-tale romance, but a woman your age doesn't expect that. We have more important reasons to get married. Stability. Companionship. There's no good reason for either of us to stay single.''

''There's him.'' Francis pointed at Flint. The air inside the barn had cooled until it had an icy edge to it, and someone had dimmed the lights for slow dancing. A song of love betrayed was filling the barn with a quiet sadness, and more than one couple moved closer together.

''Him?'' Sam looked at Flint like he suspected

him of being part of a police lineup. "What's the
FBI got to do with anything?"

"It's not the FBI. It's him. He's my husband,"
Francis whispered.

"You're joking." Sam looked at Flint again and
then dismissed him. "You don't even know him."

"I used to know him. We were married twenty
years ago."

"Oh, well, then," The man visibly relaxed. "He's
your ex-husband."

Flint didn't like the direction the conversation was
taking. "If Francis doesn't want to marry you, she
shouldn't. And there's no reason she should ever
settle for companionship."

"If you're her ex, you have no say in this at all."
Sam looked Flint over like he had been pulled out
of that police lineup and pronounced guilty. "Besides, I'm sure she's realized by now that I'm the
kind of husband that she should have. Solid. Steady.
A man like you is okay for a woman when she's
young— What we don't do when we're young."
The man gave a bark of a laugh. "Why, I was in a
protest march myself once— But that was then and
surely by now Francis knows your kind doesn't hold
up too well over the years."

"My kind? What do you know about my kind?"
Flint forced the words out over his clenched teeth.

"I know you left her," Sam said calmly. The
brown-suited man looked smug and confident. He

glanced at Francis indulgently. "I know Francis and she'd stick by her word. So I know it's you who left."

"She was young. And scared. And me— I must have seemed like some wild guy back then. I can't blame her for having second thoughts." Flint gave a ragged laugh. "I would have left me if I'd had a choice. I was mad at the world for letting my parents die. Mad at school. Mad at friends. Mad at God. The only good thing about me was Francis. I can't blame her for leaving me."

"But I didn't," Francis said softly. "I didn't leave."

Flint snorted. "That's not what the sheriff said."

"I wasn't the one who had you arrested." Francis said the words carefully. She felt like she was walking some very important, invisible line. She tried to take a deep breath, but failed. "It was my father."

"But the sheriff said—"

"My father may have lied to him." Francis was almost whispering. They seemed to burn their way up through her throat. "I waited for you to come back that day."

Flint heard the words and stared at Francis. He shook his head like he was clearing his ears. What was she saying?

"But—" Flint took one more stab at understanding. He could see in her eyes that she was telling him the truth. "But there were papers—divorce papers—"

"Had I signed them?"

Flint shook his head slowly. "I thought you'd sign them when they were given to you."

Flint still remembered the pain of seeing those papers. At first, he'd refused to sign them, pushing them away when the sheriff brought them to his cell. But on the third day, he'd decided to give in. The sheriff said Francis was pleading with her father to get the papers signed, that she was not eating she was so upset. He couldn't bear for her to be upset. He'd bruised his fist by hitting the wall of that cell after he'd finally shoved the signed papers through the bars to the sheriff.

"You were begging me to sign them."

Francis shook her head. "No."

Sometimes the world tips on its axis. Sometimes it rolls completely over. Flint's world rolled over so many times he didn't know which side was up. "I don't understand. Are you saying that you never signed those papers?"

"I never even knew they existed," Francis said softly. "I suppose my father meant to give them to me. But I left before long and—no, I never saw the papers."

"But then—"

Francis nodded. "We're still married."

Somehow the music had stopped again, and everyone was listening.

"Well," Mrs. Hargrove finally said softly. "Well, if that don't beat all."

At the edge of the crowd...

The old man slipped into the barn unnoticed. He knew he shouldn't be here. Knew one of those knuckleheads the boss had hired to do the job tonight might recognize his voice or the angle of his chin. The disguise he'd worn when the boss talked to them out at the deserted Redfern place might not hold.

But he'd tired of watching the horse, waiting for that FBI agent to return. The old man had spotted the agent snooping around Dry Creek several days ago, but he hadn't wanted to risk making himself known by trying to get rid of the man.

He hadn't even told the boss about the agent. He was scared of the boss and was afraid the boss would want him to do something to the agent. Something dangerous. When the boss had come to town a year or so ago, he'd been friendly. The boss had seemed to understand that the town of Dry Creek owed him. But now the old man wasn't so sure. The boss wasn't friendly anymore when he called. He kept asking the old man for more and more information.

And it was dangerous.

The old man hadn't figured on the FBI getting involved. The FBI made him nervous. The old man had always figured that the only lawman he'd have to outsmart was Sheriff Wall.

But this agent was a lot brighter than Sheriff Wall. The old man was afraid the agent already suspected something.

The old man couldn't afford to be caught. Couldn't afford to go to jail or have a trial. He didn't think he could bear to speak in front of that many strangers. Why, they put a dozen people on a jury. He didn't talk to a dozen people in a year. And he never gave anything like a speech. No one would ever understand that the town of Dry Creek owed him. No, he couldn't risk getting caught.

The old man knew he couldn't stay in this town. But he didn't know how to leave, either. He didn't drive his old pickup anymore. The tires had long since flattened into pancakes, and he just let them sit. Sometimes, when the mood took him, he'd sit in the battered pickup and listen to the news on the radio. But he didn't drive.

Mrs. Hargrove did his weekly grocery shopping for him, and she'd always been willing to do an extra errand or two for him. But he could hardly ask her to drive him to Mexico.

Chapter Five

Flint sat on the edge of the steps going into the barn. The moon was still high in the night sky. A slight wind was blowing. He'd give odds that a blizzard would roll off the Big Sheep Mountains before dawn. He could hear the sounds of the townspeople inside cleaning up after the party. He'd just sent the three would-be kidnappers off with the sheriff. He wished he had a cigarette, even though he hadn't smoked in ten years.

The door opened, and Mrs. Hargrove stepped out. "There's a cup of coffee left." She had a jacket draped over her shoulders and a mug in her hand. "Thought you might want it. It's from the bottom of the pot so it'll be strong."

"Thanks." Flint smiled at the woman as he

reached up for the cup. "The stronger the better. I don't expect to sleep tonight anyway."

"I wouldn't suppose so," Mrs. Hargrove agreed as she sat down beside him. "It isn't every day you discover you're married." She smiled at him kindly. "You should be sitting here with your wife, not me."

Flint snorted. "My wife took off in a puff of exhaust fumes. Back to her brother's place with her fancy fiancé."

"Well, I expect it will take some getting used to—the whole idea."

Flint looked at her in astonishment. "She's not getting used to the idea. Didn't you hear her? She's practically engaged to what's-his-name."

"Engaged isn't married," Mrs. Hargrove replied calmly. She pulled her jacket around her more firmly, and Flint was reminded of a general preparing for battle. "It's you she's married to in the eyes of the Lord."

Flint bit back his retort. Even a general didn't always know which battles could be won. "Can't imagine the eyes of the Lord will stop her from divorcing me quick as she can. He seems to have been content to look the other way for twenty years. Why break His record now?"

"Why, Flint Harris, what a thing to say—if your grandmother heard you, she'd—she'd..." Mrs. Hargrove appeared at a loss for what his grandmother would do.

Flint helped her out. He smiled. "She'd make me sit in that straight-back chair by the window while she prayed out loud asking the Lord to help me count my blessings and forgive my faults. I used to hate that more than anything. Used to ask her to just take away the keys to my pickup like normal kids."

"That would be Essie," Mrs. Hargrove said fondly. "She prayed over everything."

"She once prayed over a chicken that was sick—fool bird ate a marble." Flint could still picture his grandmother. She had unruly gray hair that she wore pushed back with an elastic headband and strong lines in her face that even wrinkles couldn't unsettle. "I'm glad she's not here to see me now."

"Oh, well, she would understand—you didn't know Francis's dad would set you up that way."

"It's not just that. It's who I am. She'd be bro-kenhearted if she saw me now."

"Essie was tougher than you think. Her heart didn't break easy. Besides, she always said it was never too late to repent. If you don't like who you've become or what you've done, it's not too late to ask God for forgiveness and start anew."

"She was wrong," Flint said as he took the last gulp of hot coffee and stood. "Sometimes it is definitely too late."

"Flint L. Harris, that's utter nonsense you're talking.'' Mrs. Hargrove stared up at Flint from her perch on the steps. ''Just because you've had a few troubles in life—''

''Troubles?'' Flint gave a wry laugh. ''Troubles were the good times.''

''Essie always worried so over you, child,'' Mrs. Hargrove said softly as she stood. ''Said you took all the bad times to heart. Like they were all your fault. Your parents dying. Even the weather—you used to fret if there wasn't enough rain to suit you.''

''Grandma needed rain for that garden of hers.''

''Your grandma got by just fine with what the Lord provided—she didn't need you to fret for her.''

Flint remembered the lines on his grandmother's face. ''I couldn't stand by helpless.''

''Ah, child.'' Mrs. Hargrove reached out a hand and laid it on Flint's arm. ''We're all helpless when it comes right down to it. We're dependent on Him for the air we breathe, the food we eat. So don't go thinking you need to do His job. The world is a mighty big weight for anyone to be carrying around—even a grown man like you.''

The touch on his arm almost undid Flint until he wondered what Mrs. Hargrove would do if he confessed what troubles had crossed his path in life. He'd seen corruption. Hatred. Evil at its finest. A man couldn't see what he'd seen in life and remain untouched.

Flint winced inwardly. He sure didn't stack up

pretty when you stood him next to a choirboy like Sam. He'd wager the man didn't even have a parking ticket to haunt his dreams.

Flint felt like an old man. He'd seen too much bad to truly believe in good anymore. He wasn't fit for a woman like Francis.

"Oh, don't let me forget to give you this." Mrs. Hargrove reached into the large pocket of the jacket and pulled out his grandmother's Bible. "She'd want you to have it."

Flint grimaced as he reached for the book. "I always regretted just leaving it there after she died. Seemed disrespectful somehow. I should have come back for it years ago."

"The important thing is that you came back now," Mrs. Hargrove said softly. "Even if it was just to do your job."

"Speaking of my job—" Flint had left the inspector inside with the last of the paperwork "I better get back to it."

The barn was almost empty. The folding chairs were neatly stacked against the wall. The crepe paper streamers were being swept into a jumble in the middle of the floor by two aging cowboys. The refreshment table was stripped bare, and that was where the inspector was sitting and filling out the last of the forms.

"I always wonder if it's worth it to arrest them,"

Flint said softly as he walked over and sat down in a folding chair near the inspector.

The inspector looked up and chuckled. "The bean counters would just add another form asking us to explain why we let them go."

"I suppose so."

"Besides, I'm almost finished. I told the sheriff I'd come by in the morning around six and we'd set up the interrogation. Should really do it tonight, but there's a storm moving in."

"Oh, I can meet with the sheriff—"

The inspector looked up from the papers and assessed him. "You haven't had a good night's sleep in days now—I can meet with the sheriff."

The heaters had been turned off in the barn an hour ago when the guests left. The air, both inside and outside, had gradually grown heavy with the promise of snow. The windows had another layer of frost gathering on them.

"Besides," the inspector continued softly. His breath clouded around his face. "You couldn't bring Francis to the interrogation."

Flint grimaced. "Trust me. I doubt she'd go anywhere with me."

The inspector nodded. "It'll be a challenge to guard her."

Flint wasn't surprised the inspector had followed his line of thinking. They'd worked together for so long they knew the routine. "She's not safe here.

Not until we arrest the man who hired those goons to do the kidnapping.''

The inspector nodded again. ''She doesn't know she's still in danger?''

Flint snorted. ''Francis? She didn't believe she was in danger the first time.''

''Too bad. If she was scared, we could get her to agree to spend some time in the jailhouse in Miles City. Protective custody. Or to at least have a twenty-four-hour guard on her. I don't like the thought of you having to guard her.''

''Me? I've guarded hundreds of folks.''

''But never your ex-wife,'' the inspector said as he laid down the pen and folded the last of the forms. ''Besides, it's not her that I'm worried about. It's you. If we weren't out in the middle of nowhere I'd ask one of the other boys to come over and guard her.''

''I can handle it.''

The inspector grunted and looked square at Flint. The older man's eyes darkened with concern. ''Just how come is it that you've never married?''

''Lots of guys in this business are single,''

The inspector grunted again. ''That's because they marry and divorce and marry and divorce. Not many never marry.'' The older man paused a minute and then shrugged. ''Well, it's your business, I guess.''

''I won't even need to see Francis when I guard

her,'' Flint said defensively. "I thought I'd just do a stakeout. Nobody needs to know I'm there."

The inspector looked up at this sharply. "There's a blizzard coming in. Folks around here say it might fall to ten below before morning. You can't play the Lone Ranger on that horse of yours tonight."

The inspector was right. Flint knew it. He just hadn't faced the truth yet. "I'm not sure Francis would let me stay in the house with them."

"That brother of hers won't be too happy, either, but he'd do anything to protect her."

Flint snorted. "Trouble is—it's me he's protecting her from."

"I'll call and give him the order," the inspector said as though that settled it. "If one of my men has to go out there on a night like this, the least Elkton can do is to let you inside the house."

The chair in the Elkton kitchen was comfortable enough for sitting, but not comfortable enough for sleeping. Flint wondered if that was why Garth had pulled it out of his den begrudgingly when Flint had shown up at one o'clock in the morning. The inspector had made the arrangements and Flint only had to tap lightly on the kitchen door to have it opened by Garth.

"Thanks for coming." Garth ground the words out reluctantly. "It wasn't necessary, though. The boys and I can keep Francis safe."

"Like you did tonight?"

Garth grunted. "If you hadn't taken off with her like a wild man, she would have been all right."

"She would have been kidnapped. Maybe worse, with those goons."

The two men measured each other for a moment with their eyes. Garth was the first to look away. "Like I said—thanks for coming."

"You're welcome."

Garth reached behind him and pulled a floor lamp closer to the chair. He snapped the light on. "I've turned the heat down a little, but you should be warm enough. I've brought a few blankets down."

"Thanks."

Garth smiled. "If you get hungry, there's some cold lobster in the refrigerator."

"Thanks. I'll be fine."

Garth turned to leave the kitchen. "We've got a double lock on all the doors now, and the windows are frozen shut. I don't expect trouble."

"Good."

Garth looked at him and nodded before he started up the stairs.

Flint settled into the chair. He'd spent more hours lately than he wanted to count on Honey's round back, so a chair, even an uncomfortable one, was welcome. The sounds of the kitchen lulled him—the steady hum of the refrigerator, the soft meter of the clock, the low whistle of the blizzard as it started to blow into the area.

Only a fool would be out on a night like tonight, Flint thought as he relaxed. The boss of the rustling outfit wouldn't be able to get replacement men into Dry Creek until at least tomorrow. Tonight they were safe.

Flint half woke while the light was so new it was more black fog than anything. Sometime in the night, he'd left the discomfort of the chair and slept, wrapped in several wool blankets, on the kitchen floor. He'd unstrapped his holster gun and laid it beside his head. He'd used his boots for a pillow, even though, with his six-foot-three frame, that meant his toes were sticking out the end of the blankets. He wondered if he wouldn't have been better to have left the boots on his feet for the night. His dreams hadn't merited a pillow, anyway. He'd tossed and turned, chasing faceless phantoms across a barren landscape until, somehow, the face of Francis appeared and his whole body rested.

The air snapped with cold. Frost edged its way up the windowpane nearest him. But, cold and miserable as it was, Flint woke with one thought drumming through his head—he, Flint L. Harris, miserable man that he was, was married to Francis Elkton. Legally married to her. That had to count for something.

He had a sudden urge to get up and go pick her

some flowers like he'd done in that long-ago time.
Yellow roses were her favorite. He could almost picture her smelling a bouquet of roses. He decided to
close his eyes and let his mind go back to dreaming
for a few sweet minutes to see if the face of Francis
would return.

Francis hadn't slept. The moonlight filtered in
through the small frosted windows in her bedroom.
She had lain in her bed and counted the stripes on
the faded wallpaper of her old bedroom until she
thought she'd go crazy. In the past, counting had
always calmed her so she could sleep.

When the counting didn't work, she'd mentally
made a list. List making was good. She made a list
of the groceries they would need to buy to make
lasagna for everyone some day this week. With Sylvia, the kids from her youth center and the ranch
hands, they were feeding forty-some people at each
meal. Planning ingredients required arithmetic and
list making. Francis spent fifteen minutes figuring
out how much mozzarella cheese they would need.
It didn't help.

Thinking of cheese reminded her of Sam. She
didn't question why. She grimaced just remember-
ing him. She supposed he was peacefully sleeping
downstairs on the living room sofa. What was she
supposed to do with the man? He couldn't have
shown up in her life at a worse moment. With luck,

he'd see reason in the morning and catch a flight back to Denver.

And Flint—she was still reeling from the knowledge that she had actually been married to him for the past twenty years.

When they'd gotten back to the ranch last night, Garth had gone into the den and pulled out an old business envelope. Francis's name was handwritten on the outside of the sealed envelope, and Garth explained that before he died their father had given it to him to give to Francis when she became engaged. Garth had always assumed it was a sentimental father-to-daughter letter. It wasn't.

Francis had left the whole envelope on the kitchen table. She'd opened it enough to know the contents were the old divorce papers.

No wonder she was unable to sleep, Francis finally decided around four o'clock. Her whole life had turned upside down in the past twelve hours. She'd seen Flint again. She'd found out he was her husband. She'd thoroughly embarrassed herself to the point that he felt he had to kiss her to save her pride. She'd felt both sixteen and sixty at the same time. It stung that the only reason he was even here in Dry Creek was that he had a job to do. At least she'd had the decency to come back here to mourn their lost love. He hadn't even come back to pick up his family's Bible.

Finally, the darkness of the night started to soften.

The hands on her bedside clock told Francis it was almost five o'clock. She'd given up on sleep, and she got out of bed and wrapped a warm robe around her. She might as well set out some sausage to thaw for breakfast.

She had checked last night, and there was a case of sausages in the freezer downstairs. There were one hundred and sixty links in a case.

If Francis hadn't been dividing the number of sausages by the number of breakfast guests, she would have noticed there was something a little too lumpy about the pile of blankets that someone had left on the kitchen floor. But she hadn't wanted to turn on any lights in case they would wake Sam in the living room. She was used to the half-light of early Montana mornings.

Her first clue that something was peculiar about the pile of blankets was the whispered endearment, "Rose." She recognized the voice even as she was tripping on a blanket corner—or was it a boot—and was falling square into the pile of—

Umph! Chest. Francis felt the breath slam out of her body and then felt her chin solidly resting on a man's chest. She groaned inside. Even if she didn't know the hoarse voice, she'd recognize that smell anywhere—half horse and half aftershave. She moved slightly, and then realized her dilemma. Her elbows were braced one on each side of Flint's chest, and her fuzzy chenille bathrobe was so loosely tied that, if she raised herself up more than an inch or two, any man from Flint's perspective, if he opened his eyes, would see her navel by way of her chin and all of the territory between the two.

Not that—she lifted her eyes slightly to confirm that his eyes were closed—not that he was looking.

Francis studied his eyelids for any betraying twitch that said he was really awake and just sparing them both the embarrassment of the situation. There was none.

Francis let out her breath in relief. A miracle had happened. He hadn't woken up when she fell on him, and if she moved lightly, she would be up and off of him without him even knowing she'd fallen.

The congratulatory thought had no sooner raced through Francis's mind than she had another one— only a dead man wouldn't feel someone falling right on top of him! Francis moved just slightly and cocked her head to the side. She laid her ear down where Flint's heart should be, and the solid pounding reassured her that he was alive.

Francis dismissed the suspicion that he was drunk—she would smell alcohol if that were the case. He must just be so worn out that he'd sleep through anything. She'd heard of that happening.

Flint lay very still. He was afraid if he opened his eyes Francis would stop the delightful wiggling she was doing on his chest. He'd felt the smooth warmth of her cheek as she laid it over his heart. It was sweet and arousing all at the same time. He almost couldn't keep his pulse normal. He sure couldn't keep his eyes completely closed. His eyelids shifted ever so slightly and his eyes opened a slit so that he could see the ivory warmth of Francis—he looked and almost sighed. She could pose for drawings of the goddess Venus rising from her bath.

And then everything changed. Flint could almost see the moment when the warmth of Francis turned to stone.

Francis had managed to locate the belt on her robe and cinch it tighter before she realized what she had interrupted. Flint was dreaming. A floating half-awake dream that kept him in bed even though the only pillows he had were his own boots and his mattress was nothing but hard-as-nails floorboards. A dream that sweet wasn't about some distant movie star or unknown woman. No, Flint was lying there with that silly dream smile on his face because of a woman named Rose. Rose! Suddenly, Francis didn't care if she did wake Flint up.

With the flat of her hands fully open on the floor on either side of Flint, Francis lifted herself up and none-too-carefully rolled off Flint.

"It's you." Flint finally opened his eyes and smiled.

Francis was sitting beside him, a peach-colored

fuzzy robe tied around her tighter than a nun's belt. Her hair wasn't combed, and a frown had settled on her forehead.

Francis grunted. "Yeah, it's me. I suppose you were expecting this Rose woman."

"Huh?"

"Not that you aren't entitled to dream about whoever you want to dream about—"

Francis stood up.

Flint lay there. He'd never noticed Francis's toes before—never seen them from this angle before. But right across from him, sitting as they did at eye level to him since he was flat on the floor, he marveled at them. How had he never noticed what dainty little toes she had?

"What are you doing here, anyway?" Francis demanded in a low voice. She didn't want to wake the whole household. "Who let you in?"

"Garth."

Her brother was the densest man on the face of the earth. "I guess Garth would take in anyone on a night like last night."

Flint didn't answer. He suspected Garth might draw the line at letting him in under ordinary circumstances. But he didn't want Francis to know that. "Blistering cold last night."

"Well, now that you're here you might as well stay for breakfast—I just came down to get it started."

Flint deliberately winced as he lifted his head a few inches off the floor and then fell back into the pile of blankets.

Francis took the bait and knelt beside him. "You're hurt? I'm so sorry about falling on you. I tripped and, well—" Francis had reached out and was running her hands lightly over Flint's sides. "Do your ribs feel all right?"

His ribs felt like a hammer was pounding against them, but he knew it was only his heart. Francis was bending over him and her hair was trailing against his chest. It was like being brushed with feathers. Black, glossy feathers. "It's more the sides of my back."

Francis didn't hesitate. To reach his back without him moving, she had to straddle him again and run both hands along his side.

Flint sighed. There'd been little luxury in his life. Francis's hands felt like silk—or satin—maybe even rose petals.

The sigh was a mistake. Flint knew it the moment Francis's hands stopped.

"You're not hurt at all," she announced abruptly.

Flint grinned. "Can't blame a man for trying."

"You're incorrigible," Francis scolded. She should move. She knew that. But she rather liked staring down at Flint like that. His grin made him look younger than he had since he was nineteen. Only he wasn't nineteen any longer. His early morning whiskers were brushed with gray toward his sideburns. He had a scar on his face that hadn't come from falling out of a tree. And his eyes—his eyes lived in shadows.

Francis didn't realize a tear had fallen from her eye until Flint reached up with a warm hand and wiped it away.

"It's okay," Flint said simply. He didn't move the hand that had found the tear. Instead, he lifted the other hand to cup Francis's face.

Francis heard a grumble behind her, slow and insistent. She didn't want to move. But someone else was up in the sleeping household.

"What's going on here?"

Francis's heart sank. Of all the people sleeping in the house tonight, this was the last person she wanted to have to deal with right now. "Sam."

Francis turned her head slightly, and Flint dropped his hands from her face. She felt the morning cold keenly after their warmth. Sam had plaid flannel pajamas on, and still he had two blankets wrapped around his shoulders.

"There's no need for you to be up." Francis hoped he would take the hint. "Let the house warm up a little first."

Sam grunted. If he heard the hint, he didn't heed it. "What's going on?"

Francis sighed and moved so that she no longer straddled Flint. "I tripped and fell."

Only a blockhead would buy that explanation, Flint thought in bitter satisfaction. He and Francis had been seconds away from a kiss. Surely, it had been obvious.

"Oh." Sam seemed uncertain. He didn't sound convinced, but he apparently didn't want to challenge Francis. "Well, I need to talk to you."

"Can't it wait?" Francis asked as she adjusted all of the chenille in her robe until she looked more respectable than a grandmother. Once she was adjusted, she glanced at Flint again a little shyly.

Flint noticed the pink in her cheeks even if the blockhead Sam didn't.

"Francis is busy now," Flint offered. "You can talk to her later."

Flint had a problem in life—he didn't know when to quit fighting a battle. Sometimes, like today, it cost him. He saw it right away in the way Francis's chin went up and her eyebrow raised.

"No one answers for me. I can talk now."

Flint knew he needed to backtrack. Francis wasn't a woman who liked being told what to do. He rolled his blankets around him closer like he was contemplating going back to sleep. "Yeah, I won't be in the way."

Sam started to puff up. "I want to speak to Francis alone. I am, after all, her fiancé."

"Well, that's a problem," Flint said lazily. "Because technically I'm still her husband."

Sam puffed up in earnest. "I doubt that marriage is even valid anymore."

"Don't count on it," Flint said as he stood.

"Please—" Francis started to scold the two men. She fully intended to. She just hadn't counted on Flint standing up right at that moment. Sam was wrapped in plaid flannel and gray wool blankets. He looked like an overgrown boy. But Flint—Flint looked every inch a man. His shirt was unbuttoned and half off his shoulder. Francis had seen his chest muscles when she'd fallen on top of him, but nothing prepared her for the majesty of him standing there. The sight of him made her mouth grow dry. It also made her cranky. "I can talk to whomever I want to talk to."

Flint nodded and smiled. He wasn't going to lose the war on this one just because he couldn't give in on a battle or two. "Of course you can."

Chapter Six

Flint took his time walking down the stairs. There were creaks in steps fourteen and nine. He'd have to remember that. He had taken Francis's hint and left her alone with Sam so that the two of them could talk. For precisely seven minutes. In his opinion, they'd had twenty years to do their talking, and seven minutes was long enough for whatever Sam had to say.

"Where's Francis?" Flint could see into the kitchen from the bottom of the stairs. Someone had finally turned a small light on over the sink, and it outlined the kitchen appliances. The clock over the refrigerator was illuminated, and the hands shone at half past five o'clock. Early morning still in most places, he thought.

"You and I need to talk." Sam ignored the question. He had wrapped the blankets around him more closely and smoothed back his hair. He cleared his throat like he was ready to give a speech, and Flint's heart sank. "We need to settle some things—"

"You and I don't have anything we need to settle," Flint said mildly as he turned so he could see into the living room. Maybe Francis had gone in there. She certainly hadn't gone up the stairs.

"Francis and I think—" Sam persisted.

"Francis asked you to talk to me?" Flint turned.

The words sliced through the air one syllable at a time. Flint didn't raise his voice. In fact Sam had to lean forward to hear the words clearly. But even in their quietness, the words made Sam Goodman stumble and step back.

"Well, we—"

"You didn't answer my question. Did Francis ask you to talk to me?"

"Well, we—"

"And just where is Francis, anyway?" Flint had finally looked completely around.

"She went out to gather the eggs for breakfast."

"Outside! You let her go outside alone!"

Flint didn't breathe again until he stood in the open door of the chicken coop beside Garth's working barn. There was Francis. She was all right. Well, as all right as one could be in a chenille bathrobe and men's boots in the freezing morning after a blizzard.

"Don't do that again." Flint strapped on the gun holster he'd grabbed on his way out the door. He'd run to the chicken coop, following the footprints in the snow. He'd known the footprints could be a decoy—that a clever kidnapper could have set up an ambush for him. But he ran anyway. The air was so cold his breath puffed out white smoke.

Francis looked up. This wasn't her morning. Every time she turned around there was a man looking at her like she was doing something wrong. "I'm only getting the eggs."

Francis slipped her hand under another laying hen and found a warm egg. The chickens weren't used to being visited this early, but they'd behaved with remarkable poise. Maybe it was so cold they weren't interested in protesting. "Sixteen so far."

She wished she'd stopped to do more than comb her hair this morning. The cold would have added pink to her cheeks, but it was an uneven redness and she wished she'd put on some foundation. Or some eyeliner. Her eyes tended to disappear without eyeliner.

She knew she didn't look as good when she first woke up as Flint did. His rough whiskers and tousled brown hair made him look rugged, especially with the morning light starting to shine behind him.

"You are not to go out by yourself." Flint leaned

against the doorjamb and said the words clearly. "If you want to go get eggs, I'll take you."

Francis slid her hand under another warm hen. There were several dozen laying boxes in the chicken coop, each stacked on top of another. Every hen had her own nest lined with straw. Francis had looked around earlier to see where the rooster was, but she hadn't seen him. He had been unusually aggressive lately, and she always tried to check on him when she entered the coop.

"You're not still worried about me! You caught the kidnappers."

"We caught the goon guys," Flint explained patiently. Why would the sight of a woman plucking eggs from beneath those sleeping chickens affect him like this? "We still don't know who the local contact person is—and we're a long way from catching the boss of the whole operation."

"Well, certainly they won't want me. I'd think by now they'd give up."

"We're not dealing with juvenile delinquents here. They aren't likely to be distracted just because some little guys in the operation get taken in. No, they'll stay with it. They're in this deep already."

"But what am I supposed to do?" Francis laid the basket of eggs on a shelf and turned to face Flint completely. "I can't live my life in a bubble and you can't guard me forever."

Want to bet? Flint thought. "You can take reasonable precautions."

"I do take reasonable precautions. I've been trained by the City of Denver in hostage survival. And how to deal with a terrorist. I'm as prepared as any average citizen could be."

Flint didn't want to tell her how many average citizens were dead today. "Humor me. Until we find the local informant, I intend to guard you."

"But—"

"No argument. That's the way it's going to be."

"But what about—"

"Don't even ask about Lover Boy inside there. He can wait to be alone with you."

"He's not—"

Flint held up his hand. "And another thing. You're going to have to tell me you want that divorce. If you're so set on getting divorced from me, I'd at least like the courtesy of hearing it from your own lips this time."

"Who said—"

"The envelope's on the kitchen table. Still has the coffee stain from twenty years ago—"

In the shadows of the chicken coop Flint could see that Francis looked tired and worried. All of the vinegar went out of his anger.

"I just think you should ask me this time. Tell it to me straight."

Francis watched Flint turn polite. The brief hope

that she'd felt when Flint stormed into the coop died. He didn't intend to fight their fate. "I see."

"It was mostly my fault anyway. I had no business asking you to marry me. I figure your dad knew that."

Francis felt every one of her thirty-eight years.

"You'd be better off with someone like Sam anyway," Flint rambled on. *You can stop me anytime.* "He'll give you a stable home and—and—ficus. He seems like a decent enough person. Steady."

"Yes, he's steady all right." Francis didn't like the direction this conversation was going. Flint might be totally indifferent to her, but she didn't want him to encourage her to marry another man. She didn't know why he even needed to pretend to care about who she married. And then it hit her. He had his Rose. He probably wanted that divorce. "You don't need to worry about me. I don't intend to press you on anything. You're completely free."

Completely free. The words echoed in Flint's ears. Why did they have to sound like a prison sentence? "I'm not worried."

"Well, you don't need to be," Francis repeated as she gathered herself together. It had been twenty years, for pity's sake. She searched in the pocket of her robe for a hair clip and found one. She was a middle-aged woman and needed to start acting her age.

Francis reached up, twisted her hair into a tidy

bun and then clipped it into place. "I'll finish getting these eggs in and fix you some breakfast."

Flint's throat was dry. "Don't bother just for me, unless the others are getting up."

Francis picked up her basket again and returned to her task. "They'll be up soon enough. I may as well get all the eggs."

Francis knew her eyes were blurry. She told herself firmly it was because of the dust in the chicken coop. All that grain and straw made for dust. Dust led to allergies and red eyes. It certainly wasn't tears that made it hard for her to see.

Francis slipped her hand under another feathery body.

Flint had turned to look outside the coop door. A white expanse of smooth snow covered the area around the ranch outbuildings. The only footprints were the ones he and Francis had made. The thick snow made the silence even more pronounced, and it blanketed the low foothills that led up to the Big Sheep Mountains.

Flint was too relaxed. That's what he told himself later.

The indignant screech of the rooster awakened his instincts. Animals were often the first to notice danger. He turned as the feathered black bird half-flew out of the box it had been occupying.

Francis screamed.

After looking at the snow, it was hard for Flint to

see clearly when he turned to look inside the coop. White dots swam in front of dark shadows. He couldn't swear there wasn't something in some corner. Something that black rooster had just noticed. He didn't have time to even look closely.

Years of training kicked in, and Flint took four giant steps toward Francis and wrapped his arms around her before rolling with her to the floor of the coop. Once they hit bottom, he turned so that his bulk would take any bullet that might come from any corner.

Francis couldn't breathe. She forgot all about being a middle-aged woman in a fuzzy bathrobe. Her heart was beating so fast she could be inside the pages of a French spy novel. She could only see the bottom half of Flint's face, but any doubts she had about the danger she was in faded. Flint was stone-faced serious. Deadly, almost. He truly believed someone might still be after her. He'd pulled the gun out of his shoulder holster.

Dear, Lord, someone could really be after me! The realization rose like a prayer to a God she rarely thought of anymore. She wished she had stayed closer to Him. Maybe then this panic wouldn't send her emotions skittering around.

Francis wasn't prepared for the panic she felt. The training sessions she'd had about hostage situations didn't come close to preparing her. "They can have my money."

Flint looked down. Francis was lying on her back beneath him. The clip had fallen out, and her hair spread around her face like black silk. He hadn't realized he'd scared her. "Where's that fool rooster going to spend your money?"

"It's just the rooster?" Francis started to breathe again.

"Looks like." Flint choked back the rest of the reassuring words. He'd spoken too soon. He heard a sound. Outside. The soft crunch of a foot on snow. Very soft. But there. Definitely there. He shouldn't have given in to the urge to reassure Francis. Unless that rooster wore boots, they were not alone out here.

"Shh." Flint mouthed the warning silently.

Francis felt the coil of Flint's body. Every muscle was alert even though he hadn't moved. Francis willed her body to shrink. She'd heard the footstep, too. It didn't seem fair that Flint was obviously using himself as a shield between her and whoever was outside the chicken coop.

There was no other footstep. Someone outside was listening.

Flint almost swore. That meant whoever was on the other side of that knotted wood wall was military trained. Not that that was necessarily a bad thing, he reminded himself. Amateurs were always more dangerous to deal with than professionals, because amateurs sometimes missed and got the wrong target.

Flint slowly moved so that he was no longer sprawled across Francis.

"Move to the corner," he mouthed silently as he jerked his head in the direction of the right corner.

If Francis went to the right, he'd stay in the middle. That way, just in case there were any bullets, she wouldn't be close enough to him to draw fire. He hoped.

Francis mutely shook her head. She didn't want to cower in some corner while Flint faced the danger alone. She mouthed, "I can help."

Flint didn't have any more time to argue with her. He knew whoever was outside would be making a move soon.

"Francis?" The low whisper came from outside the chicken coop, and Francis recognized it immediately.

"Garth?"

Flint didn't move his hand from his gun holster until he saw the dark silhouette of Garth Elkton in the open doorway of the chicken coop.

"What in blazes is going on in here?" Garth demanded.

The ground beneath her back was ice cold, but Francis didn't want to move. Her older brother had always scolded her when she'd misbehaved as a child, and she recognized the same sound in his voice today. "Nothing."

"Nothing?" Garth asked incredulously.

"I was guarding Francis," Flint explained, in his best government-business, don't-bother-me voice. It usually backed people off. It didn't even faze Garth.

"I can see what you are doing," Garth snorted. Francis's brother had obviously rushed out here in a hurry. He'd pulled on a pair of jeans, but he wore nothing over the thermal underwear that covered his chest. "There's not a square inch of light between the two of you. I don't even want to know what you are doing out here rolling around on the ground."

"You think I'd pick a place like this to seduce a woman? At five in the morning? In freezing weather?"

"I think you'd pick any place you could, Romeo. Any place. Any time. It's just that when it's my sister, you go through me first."

Francis looked at the two men and sighed. That's all she needed. A few macho games. "Garth, I'm not a child. I can take care of myself."

Garth looked at her and shook his head. "But the chicken coop?"

"I was gathering the eggs."

"At this hour of the morning?" Garth finally looked around and saw both the basket of eggs and the rooster, strutting aggressively in the corner. Garth seemed to visibly relax. "Well, no wonder you're flat on the ground. Big Ben here doesn't like to get up before the sun. I'm surprised he didn't chase you out of here."

"I think you interrupted him," Flint said. The black rooster was watching the three humans with a growing annoyance in its beady eyes. "He doesn't want to take on all three of us—at least not yet."

"Don't worry, big fella," Garth cooed to the rooster. "We can take a hint. We'll leave you to your beauty sleep."

It took Francis fifteen minutes to pick all of the straw out of her hair. She sat on a straight-backed chair in the kitchen and willed the full light of morning to arrive.

"Well, I didn't know everything was all right," Sam protested for the tenth time. "I thought I should call the sheriff. What am I to think when I hear a scream and Garth tears out of here like the place is on fire?"

Francis tried to be fair. The fact that Flint had wrapped his body around hers when he thought she was in danger and Sam had merely put a call in to the sheriff did not make Sam a coward. Cautious maybe, but not a coward.

"I can't reach either one of them. That means they're both coming." Flint paced the kitchen with his cellular phone in his hand. "I hate to have the sheriff and Inspector Kahn drive all the way out here when we've got it under control."

"But I didn't know," Sam repeated. "I would never have raised the alarm if I hadn't thought you were both in trouble."

Flint grunted. They were in trouble, all right. Not that Lover Boy had to know about it. "The rooster did make enough noise to raise the dead."

Sam nodded and pulled his blankets closer around his shoulders. "I did what I thought best."

"Of course you did," Francis reassured him. Each time she ran a comb through her hair more straw appeared. She knew what she was doing wrong. She'd given in to vanity and was using a tiny silver comb instead of the working woman's brush she would normally use. And all because Flint insisted on watching her. Well, he wasn't so much watching as guarding. But she wanted him to know she was classy. That she didn't ordinarily lounge around in a fuzzy old robe and pick straw from her hair. She hoped he noticed that the comb was real silver—it was one of her few truly elegant, feminine possessions.

"Well, I expect they'll be here any minute now." Flint nodded toward the basket of eggs on the table. "I think it's only fair that they get some breakfast when they do arrive." He looked at Sam. "You want to scramble the eggs or tackle the pancake batter?"

"Me?" The man looked like Flint had asked him to skin a snake.

"You cook, don't you?" Flint said as he looked around the kitchen. He opened a drawer and pulled out a spatula. Then he reached down and got a glass bowl off a bottom shelf.

"Well, I guess…" Sam stuttered.

"Good," Flint said as he put the bowl on the kitchen table. He hadn't cooked an egg in over a decade, but Lover Boy didn't need to know that. "The inspector likes a little cheese in his scrambled eggs. It's not good for him, but it'll put him in a better mood." Flint opened a canister of flour on the counter. "On second thought, put a lot of cheese in those eggs. It's a long trip out here and the roads are probably packed with snow. He might have had to use a shovel."

"Okay," Sam agreed and then looked at Francis sheepishly. "You'll help me?"

"She can't," Flint said emphatically. He walked toward the refrigerator to get the carton of milk. He hadn't cooked recently, but how hard could it be? He'd read the recipe on the flour sack already. "She needs to go get dressed."

That robe that Francis wore could cover a monk, and Flint would still find it attractive just because he could remember what the soft ridges of the chenille felt like under his hands. And he didn't like her to wear the robe in front of Lover Boy. Sam was slow, but he just might figure out how soft and cuddly Francis was in that robe. Then they'd really have trouble. Flint didn't think he could endure guarding Francis if Lover Boy started hugging her.

"I can put the coffee on first," Francis offered.

"Just show me where the can is and I'll get it going," Flint said.

Flint already knew where the coffee was, but he didn't mind having Francis come over and stand next to him while she reached up on tiptoes to bring the can down from its tall shelf. He could smell her perfume. It was fainter than last night and it was unmistakably mixed with the smell of chicken, but he found that he thoroughly liked it.

"Two scoops," Francis instructed as she handed the gold can over to Flint. "It says three in the directions, but it's too much."

Flint nodded. "Don't worry. We'll have breakfast ready in no time."

The smell of coffee was rich when there was a knock on the kitchen door fifteen minutes later.

"That'll be them," Flint said as he wiped his hands on the towel he'd wrapped around his waist. "Put the eggs in the skillet."

The inspector liked the extra cheese in his eggs and he didn't fuss too much about being called out on a cold winter morning. Sheriff Wall didn't complain at all.

"Glad to be away from them," the sheriff muttered when Flint apologized for the false alarm. Sheriff Wall had left his snow boots by the door and his parka on a nearby chair.

"I suppose they're rattled by the arrest." Flint sympathized. He'd grown to know the three men better than he wanted when he had them staked out. "First time for them, I'd bet."

Sheriff Wall snorted. "They ain't rattled. They keep going on about their rights."

"We read them their rights."

"Oh, those rights they have down pat. It's the other rights they're adding to the list. Some legal mumbo jumbo about humane treatment of prisoners. To them, that means a right to clean sheets. And softer pillows. And doughnuts!" Sheriff Wall stopped as though he still couldn't believe it. "Doughnuts! I asked them if they saw any all-night doughnut shop in these parts. I'd be out getting doughnuts for myself if there were any to be had within thirty miles. Told them they could have their bowl of oatmeal and be grateful for it. We don't run no four-star restaurant here."

"Doughnuts would be nice," Sam said a little wistfully. His banker look had worn off, and he looked disheveled now that he had a little flour on his pajamas and his hair was uncombed. "Don't even have to cook them."

"You're doing fine, Lover Boy. Just grate a little more cheese." Flint turned his attention to the pancake he was frying. He had poured a perfect circle of dough on the hottest place on the griddle. He'd even slipped a pat of butter underneath it. He'd done everything he could to make this pancake melt-in-the-mouth perfect. He'd timed it to the opening of the door upstairs. He smiled. He was right on target.

"Something smells good," Francis said as she walked into the kitchen.

"Good morning." Inspector Kahn smiled at Francis.

Francis had showered and washed her hair in a peach shampoo Sylvia had given her. The smell lingered, and she put on some peach hand lotion, as well. She'd scrubbed her face until her cheeks were pink and then put on a light lip gloss. She thought about putting eyeliner and eye shadow on but she didn't want anyone to think she was making a fuss. It was enough that she pulled out the ivory cashmere sweater she'd gotten for Christmas last year and put on her gold earrings.

"Sorry about the mix-up," Francis said to the inspector as she sat down at the kitchen table. She studiously avoided looking at Flint over by the stove. "I should have considered the consequences before I went out to get the eggs. I usually do, you know. I'm in planning—for cities. I know that one thing leads to another and to another."

"I know your job history."

"You do?"

"Of course," the inspector said as he raised his coffee cup to his lips. "We made brief profiles on everyone in Dry Creek when this rustling started."

"You mean I was a *suspect?*"

"Not really." The inspector gave a quick smile and looked toward Flint. "We—even Flint—figured you weren't too likely."

"Well, I certainly wouldn't steal cattle from my own brother."

"Oh, no, that wasn't the reason we ruled you out. Actually, Garth being your brother made you more likely. Maybe you had a grudge. Maybe you figure you should have inherited more when your father passed away."

"I never gave it a thought."

The inspector shrugged. "People do. In the best of families. Whether it's cattle or stocks and bonds."

"Well, Flint would know that I'd never—" Francis started to protest again and stopped. She had no idea what Flint thought of her or had thought of her for the past twenty years.

"Pancake?" Flint interrupted as he set a plate on the table that held a perfectly round, perfectly browned pancake.

"Thank you."

"Would you like some coffee, too?"

"I can get her coffee if she wants it," Sam said. The other man had left his assigned duties of chopping onions for the next breakfast shift and walked over to the table.

Flint noticed Francis wince as she got a whiff of

Sam's hands. Flint hadn't spent twenty years fighting crime for nothing. He could set someone up with the best of them.

"I've already got the pot," Flint said as he reached back and pulled the pot off the stove. "I'll take care of Francis."

"You don't need to—I've known her longer than you have," Sam said, tight-lipped. He didn't move back to the counter where he had been chopping onions. "You can't just waltz in here and take over."

"I'm not taking over," Flint said mildly. "Just doing my job. Pouring her some coffee, that's all."

"She's wearing my sweater," Sam said triumphantly as he finally turned.

"You bought her that cashmere?"

Sam nodded. "For Christmas."

Flint didn't like that. A man didn't buy a woman something as soft as cashmere without running his hands all over it, usually with the woman inside it. Flint found he didn't like the thought of Sam touching Francis. He didn't like the idea of Francis wearing that sweater, either.

"We're going to have to be going," the inspector said as he pushed his chair away from the table.

"Yeah," Sheriff Wall agreed. "Roads have been closed to everything but four-wheel drives. I should get back to the office unless anyone needs me."

"I didn't know the snow was that bad." Flint

cheered up. "You think it's high enough to keep the bad guys out for a while?"

The sheriff shrugged. "The Billings airport has been closed since last night. Even if they could fly anyone in from the west coast, they'd be stuck in Helena. And most of the rental cars would never make it to Dry Creek."

"That means I'm not in danger?" Francis asked in relief. "Flint doesn't need to keep guarding me?"

The thought of Flint leaving didn't please Francis. But she would like to know if he would stay with her even if he didn't need to guard her because it was his job.

"Now, I wouldn't say you're out of danger," the inspector said slowly as he looked at the scowl on Flint's face and then at Francis. "The odds of trouble have gone down, but they haven't disappeared. I'd say you're in danger until we figure out who the informant around here is. Until then, you'll need to be guarded."

"You mean someone who's already here is the informant?"

The inspector nodded. "Someone who has been here all along. The rustlers are getting a local tip-off."

"I don't suppose you could be wrong?"

"Not much chance."

Francis squared her shoulders and looked at the inspector. "Then we have work to do. I'm happy to help figure out who the informant is—and see if it is someone local. I'm pretty good at setting up a cross-tabbed table—if you want to look at who has been around at different times."

"You'd be working with Flint," the inspector said. "Might be good for you both."

"Oh."

Flint grunted. It didn't escape his notice that Francis was in a mighty hurry to get away from him. You'd think a woman would like a man who was spending so much effort working to keep her alive.

"Why don't you set up shop at the hardware store in Dry Creek," the inspector suggested. "I think it might be good for people around here to see that the FBI is doing something—their taxes at work, that sort of thing."

"That'd be a good place." Francis ate the last piece of her pancake. "It's more businesslike there. We won't be distracted."

And I won't be distracted, Francis vowed. There was a step-by-step path in every relationship, and she fully realized that she and Flint could not take the next step in getting to know each other again until this rustling business was settled.

"We could try the café instead," Flint offered.

"You're hungry?" Francis stood up from the table. "Of course, you probably don't like eggs and pancakes—I can fix—"

"I like pancakes just fine," Flint protested as he

waved her back to her chair. "I just made batter for another dozen more."

"Well, then, why go to the café?"

"A café has candles," Flint explained wearily. "I thought we'd like a candle on the table."

Now she understood, Francis thought. Flint wanted to burn any paper they wrote on right at the table. Her face blanched. He was right, of course. There could be an informant around any corner. A dangerous informant.

Flint sighed. He hadn't made that many romantic suggestions to women in the past few years, but he couldn't believe it was a promising sign when the woman's face went ten shades whiter. Times couldn't have changed so much that a candlelit dinner—or lunch—wasn't considered romantic.

Chapter Seven

The café wasn't open yet so Flint had to content himself with taking Francis to the hardware store. It was nearly impossible to date someone in a place like Dry Creek. Especially when the woman you were dating didn't know you were courting her. All this talk of crime didn't set a very romantic mood. And a hardware store! There wasn't even a dim light anywhere. At least not one that wasn't attached to a fire alarm.

Flint was tempted to ask the clerk behind the counter if he could borrow the small radio he had plugged in by his stool. They might get lucky and hear a country-and-western love song. But the clerk was Matthew Curtis, a minister who had recently gotten married and was probably in some romantic haze of his own.

Matthew had married Glory Becker, the woman who had become famous locally as the flying angel in Dry Creek's Christmas pageant. Flint hadn't been in Dry Creek then, but he'd read reports. He'd even heard the gossip about how the angel had brought the minister back to God. A man like Matthew wasn't likely to let folks listen to anything but hymns, and that sure wouldn't help a man's courting.

But that wasn't the only reason Flint hesitated. Flint was reluctant to ask a minister for anything, even a minister who was now a clerk in a hardware store. Flint half expected the man to question him about the Bible Flint still carried with him. Flint knew he could have left the book in the pickup he had borrowed from the inspector, but he didn't. He liked having his grandmother close by—wished she were here now with her brusque no-nonsense approach to life.

"It couldn't be number twenty-six," Francis announced as she consulted the notebook she'd been writing in all morning. She'd given each person in Dry Creek over the age of sixteen a number so that she could be more objective about them. Flint had cautioned her that children under the age of sixteen were also capable of crime, but she wouldn't listen. She insisted no child in Dry Creek could be involved. "Number twenty-four is sweet. And he wouldn't know a Hereford from a Guernsey. I can't see how he'd ever set up an operation like that. I think maybe I should delete people who don't know the cattle business, too.''

Francis wished she could delete all the suspects in Dry Creek. It made her feel old to realize that someone she had known all her life could be stealing from the ranchers around here. Anyone from Dry Creek would know the thin line that separated some of the ranchers from success and failure. A rustling hit could mean some of them would need to sell out. Who would do that?

They were both sitting on the hard-back chairs that formed a half-circle around the Franklin stove that was the centerpiece of the store. Flint was relieved to find out that this part of Dry Creek at least was the way he remembered it. Usually, an assortment of men would be sitting around this stove sharing worries about the weather or information about crop prices. But the snow had kept them home today.

''I remember you raised a Hereford calf for 4-H that year,'' Flint mused leisurely. The snow outside would keep even the most determined villians away. The FBI had already analyzed all the people in Dry Creek. Flint knew Francis wouldn't come up with anything new. The inspector had assigned her the task so she'd have something to worry about while she was with Flint. It wouldn't have taken a tenth

of the inspector's powers of observation to see that
Francis was all nerves around him, Flint thought.
It'd take more than a fancy flowchart to make her
happy with him guarding her. "You even named
him—what was it?"

"Cat."

Flint chuckled. "Yeah, I remember now. You had
wanted to have a kitten instead, but your dad said
you were in cattle country and—if you were that set
on having a pet—it was a calf or nothing."

"It could be number sixteen." Francis looked up
from her list and frowned slightly. "I hope not,
though. He has two little kids and his wife has been
sick a lot. He needs the money, I'm sure, but—"

"You loved that Cat of yours," Flint continued
staunchly. It was real hard to strike a light note when
Francis insisted on worrying over the guilt of her
neighbors. "Bet there never was a calf like him."

"Her." Francis finally looked up from her list. "I
picked a her so that she could go on to be a mother
and have calves of her own."

Something about the tightness of Francis's voice
warned him. Francis had always wanted children.
Should have had children. That was the one dream
she'd shared with him back then. "I hadn't thought
about that—"

"It's not important."

"Of course, it's important," Flint protested. Until
now, he'd just thought of those wasted twenty years

as a trick being played on him. He hadn't had time to adjust and realize what they had meant for Francis. "You were meant to be a mother. That's all you ever wanted to be."

Francis blinked and looked at her list. "We don't always get what we want in life."

"I know, but—" Flint had a sudden flash of a little girl who would have looked like Francis. He'd never realized the sum total of his own loss until that minute. He could have had a daughter. Or a son. His life could have meant something to someone besides the FBI. "How could this all have happened?"

Francis looked at Flint. She'd been nervous all morning around him-wondering what he thought of her hair, of her clothes, of the words she spoke. All of those things suddenly didn't seem so important now as she looked at him, the defeat plain on his face.

"It certainly wasn't your fault," Francis comforted him softly.

"Well, it wasn't yours, either."

"I could have had more faith in you."

Flint snorted. "You were a kid. What did we know?"

"It was just one of those things."

"Like fate?" Flint challenged. He had fought many enemies in his life, but he'd never tackled fate before. It was like boxing with a shadow. There was no way to win. "You're saying it was our fate?"

"Well, maybe not fate, but—" Francis glanced over at Matthew and lowered her voice. She'd given this a lot of thought in the hours she'd lain awake last night. She'd remembered snatches of what she had learned in Sunday school as a child when her mother used to take her. "But it must have been God's will."

"Well, I don't think much of God then if He's got nothing better to do than mess up the lives of two young kids so crazy in love they couldn't see straight." Flint knew he was speaking too loudly for Francis's comfort. She kept looking at Matthew. "And I don't care who hears me on that one. It wasn't fair."

Francis looked at Matthew. She remembered pictures of God in his long white robes. She had never considered the possibility that God was unkind until last night. He had always seemed distant, like her father. But never unkind. "I'm sorry."

Matthew stopped polishing the old lantern that was sitting on the counter. "Don't be. I happen to agree with Flint there."

"You do?" Flint was as surprised as Francis.

Matthew nodded. "It's what drove me out of the ministry."

"So you agree with me?" Flint asked for clarification. He thought ministers always defended God.

That was their job. "You're not taking God's side in this?"

Matthew laughed. "I don't know about there being sides to this issue. I know it's not fair—" he assessed Flint "—and you—you're probably sitting there wishing there was some guy you could arrest and make pay for all of this."

Flint gave a short, clipped laugh. "There's something about an arrest that levels the field again."

"Only there's no one to arrest," Matthew continued. He walked around the counter and stepped over to the small table that had been set up next to the window. A coffeepot sat on the table, and the flavor of good coffee had been drifting through the air for some time now. Matthew turned to Flint and Francis. "Coffee?"

"Yes, thanks," Flint said as Francis nodded.

"The most frustrating thing about injustice is that usually we can't do anything about it," Matthew said as he poured coffee into three thick, white mugs.

"You're saying there's nothing we can do about bad things?" Francis asked.

"Now, I didn't say that." Matthew turned to look at them again. "Sugar or cream? Or maybe a flavor? I've got some orange flavor. Or raspberry."

"Plain for me," Francis said.

"Me, too." Flint watched as Matthew balanced

the three cups on a small tray and brought them over to where he and Francis were sitting.

"We need to get some TV trays around here," Matthew apologized as he pulled up a wooden box with his foot. "The regular clientele never was one for fussing, but lately—"

"Since Glory's been around," Francis finished for him in a teasing tone.

"Well, you have to admit she does bring a whole new brand of people into the store here." Matthew laughed and then sobered. "I'm blessed to have her in my life."

Matthew carefully set the coffee cups on the box within easy reach of both of them. "And it's a blessing I almost let get away just because I was stuck on the same problem that is plaguing you two."

"And that would be?" Flint prodded. He didn't know the ex-minister well, but he'd watched him at the wedding reception the other night. Matthew had had kind words for everyone present.

"Being so preoccupied with my anger toward God for what had happened in the past that I was totally unable to accept any blessings in the here and now."

"But you still hold God responsible?" The conversation was getting under his skin, and Flint realized he really wanted to know what the minister thought.

"Of course," Matthew agreed as he pulled up

another straight-back chair and joined them in front of the Franklin stove. "But it's not always that easy. Like for you two—you can sit there and be mad at God for letting you be pulled apart twenty years ago or you can sit there and thank Him for bringing you back together now."

"But we lost so much," Flint said.

"Maybe," Matthew said as he took a sip of hot coffee. "But I'd guess there's things you gained along the way, too. Who would you be today if you hadn't parted back them?"

"We'd be chicken farmers," Flint said, and smiled. "Living on my grandmother's old place. But at least the windows would be fixed."

"And I would have had a child," Francis added shyly and cupped her hands around her mug as though she had a sudden chill.

"Maybe," Matthew said. "But then maybe something would have happened and that child would be nothing but a heartache to you—maybe there'd be a sickness or who knows what. The point I'm making is that when God takes us down a path all He asks is that we're willing to go. He doesn't guarantee that there won't be troubles on that path. All He guarantees is that He'll walk it with us."

"That sounds so easy," Flint said.

"Doesn't it?" Matthew agreed as he set his coffee cup down. He grinned at Flint. "Trust me, it's not as easy as it sounds."

Flint reached down beside his chair and picked up the Bible he'd lain there earlier. "My grandmother tried to pray that kind of faith into me when I was here with her."

"Well, she must have succeeded," Francis said.

Flint looked at her in surprise.

"You wrote a verse next to our marriage lines," Francis explained softly. "It must have meant something to you at the time."

"I didn't write any verse," Flint said as he flipped the Bible open to the center pages where the family record was kept. He looked down and saw the writing. "It must have been my grandmother. She must have written something down. And here I thought I'd covered my tracks and that she didn't know—"

"Song of Solomon," Francis said as she stood and looked over Flint's shoulder. "Verses six and seven—chapter eight. Let's read it."

"Now?" Flint looked at the Bible.

"Why not? If your grandmother had something to say about our marriage, I'd like to hear it."

Flint shrugged and started to page through the early part of the Bible. "I guess you're right."

Flint skimmed the verses his grandmother had selected before he cleared his throat and read them aloud. "Set me as a seal upon thine heart, as a seal upon thine arm: for love is strong as death... Many waters cannot quench love, neither can the floods drown it—'' Flint's voice broke and he couldn't continue.

"Those are sweet words," Francis said softly. "I thought she might have picked something about the folly of youth or trusting strange women."

Flint smiled. "My grandmother liked you."

"She must have thought I left you, as well."

Flint looked at Francis. "We were all a-tangle, weren't we? So many if onlys—"

"It just wasn't right."

"No, no, it wasn't." Flint looked at Matthew. "You know, you seem like a good person. But I just don't see how God could let this happen."

Matthew nodded, rather cheerfully, Flint thought. "So you think He could have stopped you?"

"Stopped me?"

"Yeah, when you decided to run off to Vegas that night—you must think God could have stopped you."

"Not unless He sent in a tornado."

The door to the hardware store opened, and a blast of snowy wind blew in with the well-wrapped figure of an older woman. She had to remove two head scarves before Flint recognized Mrs. Hargrove.

"A tornado," she gasped when she could speak. "Don't tell me we're getting a tornado on top of this?"

"Of course not," Matthew assured her. "This is Montana, not Kansas."

"Well, nothing would surprise me anymore," Mrs. Hargrove muttered as she removed her gloves and set them on the counter. "Everything in Dry Creek has gone topsy-turvy these days."

"Something must be happening to bring you out in this kind of weather," Matthew agreed calmly as he walked over and helped Mrs. Hargrove struggle out of her coat. Flecks of snow still clung to the plaid wool. "Why don't you sit by the fire and tell us all about it while I get you a cup of that cocoa you like."

"Oh, it's just old man Gossett." Mrs. Hargrove started to mutter as she walked to an empty chair and sat down with a sigh. "I swear I don't know what that man is thinking."

"Mr. Gossett?" Matthew said in surprise as he turned from the coat hook behind the counter. "I've never heard anyone complain about him before—I mean except for the usual—his drinking and his cats."

"That man—I swear he's stretched my Christian patience until there's only a thin thread left," Mrs. Hargrove continued and then looked at Flint. "Oh, I'm sorry—you probably don't know him. I wouldn't want you to think he's typical of the folks hereabouts."

Flint had never seen Mrs. Hargrove so flustered. He turned to Francis. "What number is he?"

"Old man Gossett?"

"Yes."

"Why, I—" Francis was scanning her paper. "I think I forgot to put him on the list."

"Forget anyone else?"

Francis was running her finger down the column. "Let me do a quick count—no, I'm only one short."

"He's an easy one to forget," Mrs. Hargrove said with irritation still fresh in her voice. "Forgets himself often enough—as long as he has a bottle he's never seemed to care about anything or anyone."

"What's his name?"

Mrs. Hargrove looked at him blankly. "Why, Gossett. Mr. Gossett."

"His first name."

"Well, I don't know." Mrs. Hargrove frowned in thought. "He's always called old man Gossett. I try to call him Mr. Gossett myself because it reminds me he's one of God's creatures, but I don't think I've ever heard him called anything else. Just old man Gossett or sometimes Mr. Gossett."

"Didn't his father settle Dry Creek?"

"Back in the big drought in the twenties," Mrs. Hargrove said as she nodded. "Folks here talk about it sometimes—our parents and grandparents all pretty much had settled around these parts after the Homestead Act of 1902. But they wouldn't have stayed if it hadn't have been for the Gossett who was alive then. He started this town and named it

Dry Creek to remind folks that they could survive hard times. Made us a community.''

"So Dry Creek owes the Gossett family a lot?"

Mrs. Hargrove shrugged. "In a way. Of course, it would be different if it was the first Gossett. I was a little girl way back then, but I remember him still. Quite an impressive man. Never could figure out why his son didn't measure up."

"You must remember," Francis interrupted. She was chewing on the tip of a pencil. "If you knew old man Gossett when he was a boy, you must have known his name."

"Why, you're right," Mrs. Hargrove said. "It's just he's been old man Gossett for so many years— but you're right, back then he wouldn't have been—" She closed her eyes and then smiled. "Harold. It's Harold. Little Harry, they called him. Little Harry Gossett."

Mrs. Hargrove was clearly pleased with herself as Francis added the man's full name to her list.

"Now he's eighty-three," Francis declared.

"Eighty-three in what, dear?" Mrs. Hargrove leaned over to see Francis's list more clearly.

"You didn't tell us your news." Flint interrupted the older woman quickly before she could ask any more questions. He didn't relish telling her that all her friends and neighbors were suspects in aiding the rustlers. So far, most of the people in Dry Creek all believed the rustlers were outsiders, from the west coast, they figured. They would never look at their own ranks.

"Why, bless me, you're right," Mrs. Hargrove said as she straightened in her chair. "And after I hurried all the way over here."

"It's not the boys, is it?" Matthew asked in alarm.

Mrs. Hargrove smiled. "Your boys are fine. They're with Glory. It's just that Mr. Gossett— Harold—has been trying to talk Glory into driving him into Miles City, and I was afraid she'd weaken and say yes." Mrs. Hargrove looked around sternly. "I told them both no one had any business driving anywhere in weather like this and that if all he wanted was a bottle of something to keep him warm until the roads cleared he'd be welcome to my vanilla."

"I don't think a bottle of vanilla would keep him happy enough." Flint almost smiled.

"I read in the newspaper that vanilla is ninety-nine percent alcohol and alcoholics sometimes tip back the bottle," Mrs. Hargrove announced.

"Unless you have a gallon of it, though, it's not going to be enough."

"Well, Glory might give him hers, too."

Flint had a mental picture of all the ladies of Dry Creek emptying their cupboards to keep Mr. Gossett happy during the blizzard. It was neighborliness at work.

"Do you think we should be giving him anything?" Francis worried. "Maybe now's a good time for him to quit."

"He doesn't want to quit." Mrs. Hargrove grunted in disapproval. "He wants to talk someone into braving this weather just to take him to a store. Or a bar, more like it."

"I could go talk to him," Flint offered. He would like to get reacquainted with the man Dry Creek had forgotten even while he lived in their midst. "I'll tell him there's a fine for endangering lives or something like that."

"Scare him?" Mrs. Hargrove asked, but Flint couldn't tell whether or not she liked the idea.

Flint shrugged. "Just slow him down. If he can wait until tomorrow, the roads will be better."

"The wind might stop, too," Matthew offered. "The forecast says this storm will blow through tonight."

"It really is too bad he can't quit," Mrs. Hargrove said softly. "That little boy wasn't so bad, now that I remember him from all those years ago. Wonder whatever happened?"

Flint kept his hands in his gloves while he knocked on Harold Gossett's front door. Flint had convinced Francis to wait outside in the pickup for him while he spoke with Mr. Gossett. It was probably nothing, but Flint had a feeling about this man.

If anyone had a grudge against Dry Creek, he'd bet it was this Gossett fellow. He knocked again.

A shadow crossed the peephole in Gossett's front door. Funny, Flint thought, no one else in Dry Creek felt the need for a peephole. Even if they locked their doors, they just called out and asked who was outside. But you couldn't arrest someone for having a peephole in their door. If you could, all of California would be in jail. Maybe Gossett just wanted to avoid his neighbors as much as they wanted to avoid him.

The door opened a crack. The inside of the house was dark. A subdued light came in through the blinds that were drawn at each of the windows. There wasn't much furniture. An old vinyl recliner. A television that was blinking. A wooden table pushed against one wall with rows of beer bottles stacked up underneath it. The house smelled of cats, although it wasn't an unpleasant smell.

"Hi," Flint said as he took his glove off and offered his hand to the man inside the house. "My name's Flint Harris."

"Essie's grandson." The older man nodded. The man was heavyset with a looseness to his face that came from drinking too much. He was wearing a pair of farmer overalls over thermal underwear that had holes in both of the elbows. If the man was planning to go to Miles City today, he certainly wasn't worried about making a good impression once he got there.

"I wanted to introduce myself," Flint said. He was beginning to doubt his suspicions about the man. He certainly didn't look like he'd come into any money lately. Not with the way he lived. "I've tied my horse out back on the other side of your yard a few times of late."

"Ain't my property."

"I know," Flint continued. "I checked it out first. Still, I thought you might have been curious."

"Nope."

The older man started to close the door. Flint moved his foot to block it.

"Just wanted to talk to you about your conversation with Glory Becker—I mean, Glory Curtis."

Gossett's eyes jumped slightly in guilt. "I wasn't talking to her."

"That's good, because it would be foolish to try to drive into Miles City today. I was worried when I heard that's what you were planning."

The older man swallowed. "I wasn't going nowhere."

"That's good," Flint repeated. He was beginning to see why Mrs. Hargrove found the man exasperating. "See that you don't. At least not until the blizzard breaks. Nothing's that important."

The old man nodded vacantly. Flint had seen that kiss-off-to-the-feds face enough times to know that it didn't mean the man was agreeing to anything. Still, there wasn't much else Flint could do. He moved his foot so the door could close.

Francis opened the door on the driver's side so Flint could slip into the pickup.

"What do you know of Gossett's drinking style?" he asked as he turned the key to start the motor.

"He drinks lots."

"But lots of what? He's got enough beer in there to keep an army happy, but he might be out of something else. Maybe he uses beer as a chaser for hard liquor and he's out of hard liquor?"

Francis shrugged. "Must be. Why else would he be so set on going into Miles City?"

"Maybe he's out of cat food. I understand he's got lots of cats."

"Yes, but he could borrow cat food from anyone in Dry Creek. Folks often borrow back and forth in the winter months instead of making a special trip to Billings or Miles City."

"Maybe he's got a lady friend he visits?"

"Old man Gossett?" Francis asked in genuine surprise.

"Well, you never know," Flint said as he backed away from the Gossett house. At least he had Francis thinking about romance again.

"Old man Gossett," she repeated.

Well, maybe not romance, Flint thought wryly as

he started driving down the short road that was Dry Creek. She sounded more like she was thinking of a circus act.

"Oh, look," Flint said as he drove level with the café. "It's open"

A black Open sign was hanging in the window of the café under another more permanent sign that read Jazz and Pasta.

"We could stop for coffee," Flint offered.

The interior of the café smelled of baking bread and spicy tomato sauce. Black and white linoleum covered the floor, and several square tables were set up for dining.

Ah, here we go, Flint thought as he saw a small candle in the middle of each table.

"Allow me." Flint held the chair for Francis.

Now they were getting somewhere, Flint thought.

His heart sank when Francis pulled out her checklist.

"I think we need to consider thirty-four, too," she said. "He got his hair cut."

"His hair cut?"

"Yeah, and it wasn't anyone around here who did it," Francis said. "You can't get a cut like that in Miles City even—I'd say he's been to Spokane or Boise."

Flint sighed. Francis would have been a terror on the force. "You want to talk about some guy's haircut?"

"It could be important," Francis persisted. *Besides, I don't know what to say to you. I'm afraid of saying anything that's going to rock this boat we're on.*

Our lives could be important, too, Flint felt like saying. But he didn't. Maybe Francis was right. Maybe it was too late for them to go back to what they once were.

The minister, Matthew, had seemed hopeful, saying they should thank God for bringing them together now instead of being angry for being separated earlier. But even if God was bringing them together now, why was He bothering? It seemed more like a cosmic joke than anything—bring the two young lovers back together so they could realize what they had missed during all those years.

Flint let his hand drop to the Bible that sat on the seat next to him. He felt comforted just touching the thing—maybe more of his grandmother's faith had gotten under his skin than he ever realized. He had a sudden urge to pray and wished he knew how. Wished that words would form on his lips to express the confusion inside his heart. But his lips were silent.

Chapter Eight

A teenager walked out of the back of the restaurant. She was wearing a white chef's apron over faded jeans, and her shaggy hair was dyed a bright copper red. As she walked she pulled an ordering pad out of the apron pocket. She snapped her chewing gum. "Can I get something for you folks?"

"Hi, Linda," Francis greeted the teen. "How's business?"

"Not bad," Linda said and smiled. "We've decided to open for the breakfast crowd now—so far so good—we got seven breakfast orders from Sheriff Wall already this morning. We didn't have doughnuts, but Jazz makes a mean biscuit served with honey. The sheriff bought a dozen extra biscuits. Asked me to cut little holes in them so they looked like doughnuts," Linda shrugged and smiled again. "And folks around here think I'm weird because I got my nose pierced."

The teenager tilted her face so Flint and Francis could see the sparkling stud in the side of her nose.

"Nice," Flint said with a smile. Linda's face was scrubbed clean and fresh-looking.

"Just the right touch," Francis agreed. She was glad Linda had forgotten about the black lipstick she sometimes wore.

The teen took their order for coffee and biscuits and called out, "Two for a combo—make it sticky!" to someone in the back before walking over to the coffee urn that rested on the counter at the side of the large room.

"What number is she?" Flint whispered to Francis.

"Linda?" Francis seemed surprised. "Well, she's number twenty-seven, but I don't really think—"

"She's in a public place," Flint reminded her. He enjoyed watching Francis's eyes. Their gray depths had lost all semblance of calm. "Good place to get information. Overhear talk about cattle. Maybe know when a rancher is sick and not making his usual rounds."

"But the ranchers don't hang out here," Francis protested firmly. "Besides, their café has only been open since Christmas Eve. Most of the rustling happened before that."

"True." Flint liked the way Francis's eyes got

passionate in their defense of the young woman. He tried a different tactic. "How old do you think she is?"

"Eighteen, I think."

"And this Jazz guy that works the restaurant with her?"

"Duane? A year or two older."

"Just like us," Flint said softly. "That was the age we were when we got married."

The old man looked in the back window of the café. He knew that this window beside the black cookstove wouldn't be frosted up and would still be hidden from the people inside the café. He had to stand in a snowbank to get a good view through the window, but that didn't bother him. He'd be a lot colder if he didn't find a way to get to that bus in Miles City.

What were they talking about? The FBI man and Francis. She was a smart one, she was. He'd known her mother. She had been the same way. Never did understand why she had married Elkton when she could have married him. He'd been somebody back then before the drinking.

The FBI man thought he was so clever, coming to his door with some nonsense about the roads. But the old man wasn't fooled. Since when did the federal government care about cars driving in snow?

Besides, he had seen the agent look in his trash

barrel the other day and take out an empty jelly jar that had broken. The jelly was crab apple, left over from a summer when Mrs. Hargrove had canned some jelly for him from his tree. The agent put the jar back, but the old man wasn't sure if he'd taken a fingerprint off of it somehow. The agent must have. What did the government care about empty jelly jars?

It all made the old man nervous. He had to get out of town. That Glory Becker wasn't much of an angel as far as he was concerned. Wouldn't even drive him to Miles City in that Jeep of hers. And she had good tires. He'd checked them out. He'd half considered stealing them to put on his pickup, but he couldn't use a tire iron anymore. Couldn't drive his pickup even if it had tires on it, when it came right down to it. He hadn't driven anything for a good twenty years now—he'd be surprised if he'd know how, especially if he was behind the wheel of a newfangled car.

He was an old man, plain and simple. He was surprised the Becker woman hadn't agreed to help him. What kind of Christian charity was she showing—she just said no and kept talking about the twins. You'd think she was their real mother the way the woman went on about them. Little Joshua and little Joey. It made the old man want to gag. He knew it wouldn't hurt the little creatures to stay home alone for a day. Might even do them some good. Take some of the happy shine off their infernal faces.

Disgusting. And no help at all.

He'd have to try something else. And soon. Before any more snow got dumped on the roads and the bus got canceled.

Francis felt her nerves stretch tighter than a new drum. The day had stiffened her like a board. She was grateful Garth had convinced Sam to spend the day with some of the ranch hands in the bunkhouse. She suspected they were teaching him to play poker. If they were, he'd be there until supper trying to win his money back.

She wished she had something like that to worry over. She'd tried to keep her mind organized, but she hadn't succeeded. Her thoughts kept straying— kept going back to the wistful look on Flint's face when he realized that Linda and her fiancé, the Jazz Man, were the same age she and Flint had been when they eloped to Las Vegas.

Linda and the Jazz Man were working toward their dream. The two teenagers had sat with her and Flint after they had their biscuits and talked about the farm they planned to buy when they'd saved enough money. Their faces shone with their dream. They were halfway to their goal already. Every dollar helped. They had looked happy when Flint offered to pay them fifty dollars if they would go out to his grandmother's old place and bring Honey back to the small building behind the café so they could feed and water her for a day or two.

Francis sighed. She wished her own dreams were as simple to fulfill.

"You okay? Flint asked me to check."

Francis glanced up and saw her brother standing in the doorway and looking at her in concern. She had told Flint she was going into the den and didn't want to be disturbed. It was taxing to be guarded— especially by Flint. They'd spent the whole day together. It was almost time for supper, and Francis needed some time alone before she offered to help the others prepare the meal.

"Yeah, sure," Francis answered. "Tell Flint I'm fine."

She was sitting in the old rocker in the den. The room was growing darker as the last of the day's light seeped in through the frost-covered windows. The furniture in Garth's house had been replaced in the past few years, but the rocker was one thing that would never leave. This was the chair their mother used to sit in when she read to them when they were each small. Garth kept it in the corner of the den that couldn't be seen from the door. Francis suspected he used it as an escape place, too.

"Want to talk about it?" Garth offered as he pulled over a straight-backed office chair and sat down. "I suppose you're still mad at Dad."

Francis grimaced. "He could have told me. I spent so much time being angry with Flint. Even if Flint had gone on with his life by then, Dad should have told me."

"Probably meant to." Garth mused. "Dad was never much good at talking, and I'd guess it got harder to tell you as the years went on."

Francis hesitated and then took the plunge. "And I've been thinking about Mom, too."

Garth sat still. "Oh."

"Do you remember her taking us to church? I always remember her getting you and me ready and taking us to Sunday school and then church."

"Yeah." Garth was noncommittal.

"Why did she?"

Garth seemed surprised. "Why? I never thought about it. She just did. That was part of her being Mom."

"Do you think it meant something to her? You were older than me when she died, and I can't remember." Francis could tell it was painful for Garth to talk about their mother, but she pressed on. "I can remember her sitting in this chair about this time late every afternoon—just before she started getting supper ready and before Dad came in from the fields. She'd sit a bit and read her Bible and then pray. I know she prayed with us later, when we went to bed, but this was just her time. I haven't thought about that for years. I wonder—did she really believe it all?''

"Yeah," Garth said softly. "I think she did."

They were both silent for a minute.

"I wish she were with us now," Francis whispered. Maybe her mother would know how to untangle the feelings Francis was feeling. Maybe she'd even know how to help Francis pray to the God she herself had known so well.

"So do I, Sis. So do I."

Francis looked at her brother. She hadn't noticed how weary he was looking, either. "Troubles?"

Garth shrugged.

Francis took a shot. She'd noticed how her brother looked at the woman from Seattle. "How's Sylvia doing?"

Garth grunted.

"She likes you, you know," Francis offered softly.

Garth's wince told her she had hit the sore spot.

"She's got better things to do with her life than liking me," Garth said harshly as he stood up and pushed his chair to the desk. "She deserves someone better."

"Maybe you should let her decide that," Francis said as Garth walked toward the door.

"It's already decided. If you need me, I'll be out back chopping some more wood for winter," Garth said as he opened the door.

Francis had seen the huge stack of wood Garth had already chopped in the last two days. "Don't we have enough wood?"

"Not enough to suit me."

Francis nodded. It looked like she wasn't the only one in the family with troubles in love.

Flint was in the kitchen pacing. The hands on the clock over the refrigerator seemed to crawl. What was Francis doing, locked in the den like that? He knew she had looked more and more strained as the day wore on, but he wished she would talk to him. The fact was, if she didn't come out soon, he was going to go right in and demand that she talk to him. Yes, he said to himself, that's what he'd do. It was his duty, after all. He was guarding her. On official government business. He had a right to know how she was.

Flint looked at the clock in exasperation. Two minutes down. He was beginning to understand why the inspector didn't want him to serve as guard to Francis. Being around her all day was doing things to him that he wasn't able to control. Before he knew it, he was going to make ten kinds of fool of himself doing something like demanding she talk to him. He'd never demanded that someone in protective custody talk to him before—at least not about their feelings. The FBI didn't care about feelings. It worried about the who, where and when questions.

Flint looked at the clock. One more minute. Ah, there she comes. Flint heard the faint click of the doorknob and turned to face the small hall that led to the den.

"Relax. It's just me," Garth said as he walked through the open door.

"Oh."

"She'll come out soon," Garth offered gruffly as he walked over to the rack of coats that hung near the kitchen door and pulled a jacket off a peg. He turned back and looked at Flint squarely. "Don't leave her this time."

"I never left her the first time," Flint protested and then smiled. This was as close to a blessing as someone like Garth would give him. "You don't have to worry. Francis isn't that interested in me these days. I'm only her guard."

Garth grunted as he pulled on the jacket. "I've officially turned down the FBI's request, you know. There's no reason to kidnap her."

"The bid has already been put out," Flint explained. He'd gone over that in his mind, too. "If it's put out with a crime syndicate, it's probably too late to pull back the orders. There might have been a backup in place before we even arrested those other goons."

"I'll tell the boys to keep their eyes open."

"I'd appreciate that."

A rush of cold air entered the kitchen as Garth

opened and then quickly closed the outside door. The clock crawled two more minutes before Francis opened the door from the den. Flint tried to pretend he wasn't waiting for her and turned to face the wall. Ah, good, there was a calendar tacked to the kitchen wall about level with his eyes.

"Tomorrow's Sunday, isn't it?" Francis asked as she walked down the hall.

Flint scrambled to look at the calendar more clearly. "Yes, I guess it is, at that. Why?"

"No reason," Francis said as she walked over to the kitchen sink and turned the water on. "I just thought if it was Sunday tomorrow I might go to church."

"Church?"

"I mean, if that's all right with the FBI." Francis reached into a cupboard and pulled out a teakettle. "I know I'm being guarded, but it's only church. The FBI couldn't object to that."

Flint groaned. He knew the FBI would object. He'd be placing the person he was protecting square in the middle of every suspect in Dry Creek. Everyone would be rounded up under one roof with no weapons check and predictable times when everyone from the minister on down would stand for long minutes with their eyes closed. A lot could happen with all those closed eyes. A smart kidnapper could nab their victim and hustle them out the door before the prayer finished.

"I'd really like to go," Francis continued as she put the kettle under the faucet and began to fill it with water. "And you'll be there, so there's really no danger."

The easy confidence with which Francis said the latter was Flint's undoing. She trusted him. "We'd have to sit in the back row."

"That'd be fine." Francis looked at him and smiled. "I'm sort of a back row kind of person anyway—I haven't been in church for years."

"And I won't be closing my eyes when I pray," Flint assured her.

"Oh, well, surely, there's nothing to worry about at church," Francis said indignantly.

Flint didn't remind her that the hit man that had come after Glory Beckett had chosen the Christmas pageant as the place to make his attempt on her life. The way Flint heard it, it was only the quick thinking of Matthew that had saved the woman's life.

"I'll call Mrs. Hargrove and tell her to be on the lookout tomorrow for someone who is in church but doesn't usually attend," Flint said as he walked toward the telephone. That should pinpoint any problems. "I wonder if it's too late to get some kind of metal detector set up in the entrance hall."

"I don't remember that the church has an entrance hall," Francis offered. She hadn't been in the church for years, but her memories were of a large square room that opened directly onto the street.

Concrete steps led up to the double doors that opened into the main room of the church. Two rows of old, well-polished pews faced the front of the church, and tall narrow windows lined the walls. A dark linoleum covered the floor, and a strip of carpet was laid over that to cover the aisle between the pews.

"I should alert Matthew, too," Flint muttered as he picked up the telephone to dial. "Maybe he could shake everyone's hands before the service instead of after. He can do a visual check for weapons that way. Of course, we're probably okay as long as the roads stay closed." He turned to Francis. "Don't suppose you've heard the weather lately?"

"I heard Robert Buckwalter ask Garth earlier. I think that he was hoping to fly his plane out of Dry Creek." Francis grimaced at Flint. "Either that or I hear he's thinking of having more supplies flown in somehow. Tricky business. Garth said the latest forecast was for wind and continuing cold. Unless the county snowplow can get through on the roads, I don't think cars will make it through."

"And none of the rental places rent anything but cars?"

"No, Sheriff Wall checked on that—also told the places at the Billings airport to let him know if any strange men were making a fuss about not being able to rent a four-wheel drive."

"What about women?"

Francis looked at him blankly.

"They might hire a woman," Flint said softly. "In a place that doesn't expect a woman, that could be a key element of surprise. And my guess is that they'll go for a professional this time—someone who is supposed to get in and take the hostage out without attracting any attention."

"But a woman would stick out more than a man," Francis protested. "More men travel through these parts, looking for ranch jobs or following the rodeo circuit."

"Like Sam," Flint offered.

"Sam would never," Francis protested. "I can't believe you'd even think he'd be a kidnapper."

Flint shrugged. "It's probably not him. But it could be the woman that came looking for Robert Buckwalter."

Flint had already had the bureau run a check on the woman, and she sounded like she was little threat to anyone but Robert. The report he had gotten back suggested the woman was there to try and convince Robert to marry her.

Any man who could fly in a load of lobsters on his private plane to feed a bunch of inner city kids, as Robert had done, had money to spare. That meant the woman's motive was simple. She had sighted her prey.

The blonde was having problems paying back some gambling debts and she needed to raise lots of cash fast. She'd already slipped the information to her creditors that she was on the verge of getting engaged to Robert. Flint had taken a close look at that plane Robert landed several nights ago on the snowy pasture by Garth's barn. The plane was so new it still held the smell of the mocha leather seats that turned the cockpit into a relaxation center. No doubt about it. That plane belonged to a rich man.

Marriage to Robert would certainly get the blonde out of hock. But then so would doing a little favor like kidnapping someone for a crime syndicate.

"We can't be too careful," Flint said.

"Well, I can't live in a bubble," Francis said as she sat down at the kitchen table. "We can take reasonable precautions, but that's all we can do."

Flint started to dial the number for Matthew Curtis. He wondered if the minister would be willing to rope off the last two rows on one side of the church. That way Flint could keep a neutral empty zone around Francis. She probably wouldn't like it, but he would rest easier with that arrangement.

"Besides—" Francis gave a little smile "—if another kidnapper is around here they will have noticed that the woman to kidnap, if they really want to rattle Garth, is Sylvia Bannister."

Flint looked at her in question.

"I think my brother's in love," she said softly.

"Garth?"

Francis nodded. "He might not know it yet, but, yes, Garth."

Francis was even more convinced that her brother was in love when he ate supper in the bunkhouse with a few of the men instead of joining the rest of them in the house. She wondered if all men got as grumpy as Garth when they fell in love. If that was the case, she didn't have to worry about Flint. He'd been smooth and polite to her ever since he'd agreed to attend church with her in the morning. He didn't look like he had a care in the world. He certainly didn't look like a man in love.

"Pass the salt?" she asked Flint as they sat in the middle of the table, surrounded by boisterous teen-agers. The beef stew she had helped make for supper didn't really need more salt, but it was the only conversational opener that came to her mind.

"Sure," Flint said as he lifted the little glass bottle and passed it to her. "Want pepper?"

"No, thank you." Francis smiled stiffly. Well, that wasn't much of a conversation starter. At this rate, they'd never get the important conversations going. Not that the supper table was a good place to have such a conversation, anyway. Maybe they should wait until they drove to church tomorrow. Flint had already made it clear the two of them were going alone in the four-wheel-drive pickup he was driving.

Chapter Nine

The supper dishes were done, the cows were fed, and the house was dark. But Francis couldn't sleep. She lay in the single bed in the small bedroom that had been hers for her entire girlhood. When she lay there, the years evaporated and she felt just as young and insecure as she had thirty years ago. She missed her mother.

Strange, she thought, she hadn't missed her mother for years. She thought about her on holidays and sometimes when she saw a woman who had that same shiny black hair, but she never really missed her deeply. Francis had been ten when her mother died, and it seemed like such a long time ago. She had long ago firmly closed the door on those young memories of her mother.

But tonight, Francis missed her. She wished she

could ask her mother what she felt about love and happiness. And faith. Had her mother found comfort in her faith or had it been a mere duty to her?

Francis remembered their home had known laughter as long as her mother was alive. After her mother died, no one laughed anymore.

Francis felt a moment's envy of Flint because he had his grandmother's Bible and had something to hold that had been precious to her. Then she remembered that her own mother's Bible was on a shelf in the den. Like the rocking chair, Garth had never moved it even after all those years.

Francis pulled her chenille robe off the peg behind the door and slipped her arms into its sleeves. The night air inside the house was chilled, so she moved fast. She tucked her feet into fuzzy peach slippers and tightened the belt on her robe.

Once covered, she turned on the small lamp beside her bed. If she left her door open, the lamp should give enough light so that she could sneak down the stairs and pull the Bible off the shelf without waking anyone.

Sam was sleeping on the living room sofa again tonight, and she supposed Flint was in the kitchen. She had no desire to wake either one of them.

Shadows filled all the corners of the house as Francis stepped into the upstairs hallway. She always liked the house at night. Everything was peaceful and stone quiet. When she was in Denver, she missed the absolute still of a Montana night.

Francis stepped lightly down the wooden hallway. The light from her room filtered softly into the darkness of the stairway.

Creak! Flint woke from a restless sleep and stiffened. Someone was slowly walking on the stairs. He'd tested the stairs already and found creaks on steps fourteen and nine. With only one creak, he couldn't tell if the person on the stairs was going up or down. Either way, he needed to check it out.

Flint stood silently and shrugged the blankets off his shoulders. He quickly moved along the wall that led to the stairs. He heard another creak, this one closer. Good, that meant someone was coming down the stairs instead of going up. It was less likely to be an intruder.

Flint stood beside the stairs as a shape came into view. He recognized Francis as much by the smell of the peach lotion she wore as by the shape she made in her bathrobe.

He wouldn't have guessed that the sight of Francis in her bathrobe would affect him so deeply. It wasn't even that he'd like to cuddle her up to bed—and he would like to do that—it was more that he was suddenly aware of the nights of lying together in front of the fireplace and talking he had missed.

That bathrobe got to him. It certainly wasn't the

sexiest robe in the world. He'd seen his share of see-through black robes and sleek silk numbers. They were all sexier than that old robe. But the robe reminded him of the comfortable love he'd missed. The kind of love one saw on the faces of couples who were celebrating their fiftieth anniversaries. The kind of love that was for better and for worse. He'd missed it all.

"It's me," he whispered. He didn't want to frighten Francis, and she was sure to see him before she came much closer. He thought a whisper would be soft enough.

Francis yelped all the same as she turned around. "What are you doing there?"

"I heard someone on the stairs," Flint explained softly. "I didn't know if they were going up or going down."

Francis nodded. "I'm just going into the den to get a book."

"Anything I can get for you?" Flint realized he'd never spent an evening with Francis reading. He didn't even know what kind of books she liked. "A mystery? No, not for this time of night. Maybe a romance."

Francis shook her head. "The only reading books my brother keeps around are his collection of Zane Grey novels."

"We could sit a bit and read them."

Flint liked that idea. It was comfortable—the kind of thing old married couples did.

Francis shook her head. "I don't want to wake anyone." She rolled her eyes in the direction of the living room where Sam was sleeping.

"Oh." Old married couples certainly didn't have to worry about unwanted fiancés sleeping in the living room, Flint thought.

"I'll just be a minute."

Flint walked with her into the den and stood by the door while Francis reached up and pulled a large book off the shelf.

"Thanks," Francis said as she left the den. "I remembered this belonged to my mother."

"I don't remember you talking about your mother."

"I didn't."

Francis still couldn't sleep a half hour later. She lay in her bed with her mother's Bible propped up before her. She wished she'd taken the time to look at her mother's Bible earlier. Her mother had written notes throughout the book.

Next to Psalm 100, verse five—"For the Lord is good; His mercy is everlasting, and His truth endures to all generations"—her mother had written a note. "Yesterday my baby girl was born! I'm so very happy!"

Next to Matthew 5:4—"Blessed are those who

mourn, For they shall be comforted''—her mother
had written in a slower hand, ''What will my babies
do without me?''

Her mother's life was bound up in the pages of
the Bible Francis had pulled off the shelf. Her worries were all there in black and white. Her dreams
were noted. Her joys. Francis hugged the Bible to
her after reading it for a time. She'd never expected
to know her mother like this.

The sun strained to rise, and the old man sat in
his kitchen and urged it on. He'd been impatiently
waiting for morning as he sat next to his west window and polished his old hunting rifle. He'd found
a box of ammunition in a dresser drawer last night,
and it was sitting on the table ready to be loaded.

If the sun rose hot enough, maybe some of this
blasted snow would melt and someone would be
willing to drive him to Miles City today, the old
man thought. But then he remembered—it was Sunday. The only folks in Dry Creek he could count on
to do him a favor all insisted on attending church
on Sunday mornings.

He looked around his house. It was like he'd
never really seen it for years. When had the walls
gotten so stained? And those curtains. They were
little more than threads hanging from curtain rods.
He should pack some things for his trip, but he
couldn't settle on what. Finally, he pulled out the

old photo album that had belonged to his parents and put it in a plastic grocery bag. That and the rifle were really the only things he needed to take.

He was halfway to the door when he remembered the cats. What would he do about the cats? He put down the rifle and bag and opened the cupboard door. He pulled all the tins of cat food out of the cupboard and stacked them on the counter. They were all gourmet tins—chopped chicken livers and tuna. He always bought expensive cat food. Then, one by one, he ran his manual can opener around their lids. As soon as a can was opened, he sat it on the floor.

By the time he finished, he had twenty-nine open cans on the floor. He didn't pet any of the cats that gathered at his feet, and they didn't expect it. He never petted the cats. He'd been content to simply feed them.

The old man comforted himself about the cats. When people realized he was gone, they'd come and take care of the cats, he told himself. The cats would all find good homes. Surely, the people of Dry Creek would take them in.

The old man fretted until finally the sun had softened the darkness enough so that he could put on his coat, pick up his bag and gun and walk across the street to the pay phone beside the café. He'd never put a telephone in his house—couldn't abide the demanding ringing of one. But today he needed to call the bus depot in Miles City and find out if the Greyhound bus was able to get through on the roads.

The bus wasn't coming. The short phone call let him know that the bus service was canceled for Sunday because the interstate was closed until the snowplows could get through. The next bus was scheduled for Monday.

The old man swore. Monday could be too late. The more he had thought about that cocky FBI agent—coming right to his door and forcing the old man to talk to him—the more nervous he became.

He couldn't stay in Dry Creek until Monday.

The old man had a brief vision of himself driving his old pickup in the other direction, to North Dakota, without tires. The roads were covered with snow. Maybe the tire rims would get him there. He knew it was hopeless as he thought about it. Even if he got to the North Dakota border, he'd still be stranded.

He saw a cream-colored business card slipped into the door of the café, and he pulled it out of the crack. That hotshot Robert guy and someone—the man hadn't written the name clearly—had gone out to the plane. The additional supplies had been parachuted down last night, as ordered. They would be back as soon as possible.

The old man wished he was the one with the

plane. That would sure solve his problems. A plane didn't need to wait for any snowplows.

It wasn't fair, the old man decided, when some folks like Robert Buckwalter had fancy planes and a senior citizen like himself didn't have anything but his two aching feet to get himself around in good weather or bad.

And then the old man heard it—the soft whinny of a horse coming from nearby. He listened. It was coming from behind the café. Something about the mournful whinny of the horse told him that she was alone and missing her master.

He rubbed his hands together in triumph. The horse was back! That's what he needed. A horse didn't need tires, and even if the old man couldn't quite remember how to drive, the horse wouldn't care.

Francis let the sunshine filter through the thick frost on her bedroom window. She didn't need full sunshine to feel like this was going to be a good day. She felt more hopeful than she had in years. She'd connected with her mother last night, reading her mother's Bible. Something in her had softened while she read. She was looking forward to going to church this morning more than she had expected when she first announced her desire to Flint. She felt like she'd never really paid attention in church before, and now she wanted to observe everything—to see it through her mother's eyes.

Francis smelled coffee before she started down the stairs later in the morning.

Flint was dressed in slacks and a gray turtleneck and was standing by the sink sipping a cup of coffee. If he'd noticed the creaks she made walking down the stairs, he didn't comment on them.

"You're up early," Francis said as she walked to the cupboard and pulled out a cup.

Flint grinned. "I wanted to be ready in case you wanted to go get eggs again this morning."

Francis groaned. "I think I'll wait until that rooster is awake."

"Suits me." Flint set down his coffee cup and reached over to pick up the leather shoulder holster that was on the counter. The holster was snapped shut, but the butt end of a gun was clearly visible. He hooked it over his shoulder.

Francis heard the hard footsteps on the hallway floor before she saw the outline of Sam entering the kitchen.

"You're wearing a gun to church?" Sam gave a pointed, reproving look in Flint's direction.

Flint felt the joy of the morning harden. Sam looked all starched and pressed. Since when was Sam planning to come to church with them? "I'm on duty."

"Flint's been kind enough to agree to let me attend the services," Francis said stiffly. She had never noticed before just how much of a pain Sam was. Had he always been this self-righteous? "It's been a lot of extra work, especially since he still has his responsibilities."

Sam grunted and adjusted his silk tie. "I doubt there will be many people at the service anyway, the way the snow has covered the roads."

"I've checked with the sheriff," Flint said. "The roads are passable with a four-wheel drive."

Flint had made arrangements for the sheriff and the inspector to both attend the services. One man would sit on each end of the pew where he and Francis sat.

Sheriff Wall had said he didn't usually attend, but he'd wanted to go and check the furnace in the old church, anyway. He was somewhat of a self-taught electrician, and the folks of Dry Creek often called on him for an odd piece of electrical work. He'd told Flint he'd check out the furnace early Sunday morning. That way he'd be there to see if anyone was snooping around the church building before the regular members got there.

"Anyone want some toast?" Flint said as he slipped two slices of bread into the toaster.

"I thought I'd take Francis to breakfast in Dry Creek before church," Sam said smugly as he adjusted his suit jacket. "Give her a break from all of this business."

Flint pushed in the button on the toaster. He studied Sam out of the corner of his eye. The man's face was innocent as a lamb's. But that didn't mean he wasn't capable of betraying someone. Flint wondered if someone could have gotten to Sam. The man certainly seemed intent on getting Francis away from anyone's protection. "You can take her to breakfast when we've caught all the rustlers. Until then, you'll just need to be patient."

"Of course," Sam said smoothly. "I wouldn't want to do anything that would put Francis in danger. Although—" Sam paused "—she wouldn't be defenseless with me around. I have my cell phone. I could call the sheriff in a heartbeat."

Flint grunted and bit back his words.

"Anyone like jelly on their toast?" Francis asked from the corner of the kitchen where she was bending to examine the shelves in a lower cupboard. "The kids have used all of the jelly Garth had, so Mrs. Hargrove brought us some she had canned." Francis pulled up a jar. "I think this is apple jelly."

"Does everyone around here make their own apple jelly?"

"Well, maybe not everyone." Francis opened the jar with a pop to the lid. "Some folks make chokecherry jelly instead—or rhubarb jam."

Flint let himself imagine what it would be like to live in a place where everyone had the time to make jelly. It certainly wasn't anything like the cities he'd lived in over the past ten years, where people didn't even take the time to smear jelly on their toast let alone make the stuff.

"I'll have my toast dry," Sam said as he sat down at the breakfast table. "I wouldn't want to get jam on my suit."

For once Flint was glad he could claim official business. He wouldn't have to offer Sam a ride into church with him and Francis, and in ordinary circumstances there would be little he could do to avoid it.

It was an hour later before it was time to leave for the church service. Garth and all of the kids had had a pancake breakfast while Francis was upstairs taking a shower and getting ready.

Francis lingered in the hot spray of the shower. The air inside the house was cold even though the steam from countless showers upstairs and the cooking downstairs were warming it up. When Francis stepped out of the shower, she wrapped a thick towel around her head and quickly slipped into her robe for the dash to her room.

She might as well not have dashed, Francis thought. Ten minutes later, she was still shivering, standing in front of her closet, wondering what to wear.

Her problem was one of image. She wanted to look competent—to show Flint that he didn't need to worry about her safety—but she also wanted to look appealing. A man like Flint must have dated many women in the years since she'd known him. Probably sophisticated women, too. The kind of woman who finds it exciting to date someone who wears a gun. The kind of woman who, if she wore a robe at all, wore a silk and lace one instead of a fuzzy one.

Francis sighed. Her navy striped suit was the obvious choice for competency, but it seemed a little needlessly drab. Not feminine enough. It was, however, the kind of suit that made up the endless parade of suits she'd worn for years in her job. And it was the kind of suit that filled her closets in Denver, and here, as well.

The only truly feminine dress she owned was the long ruby evening gown she had worn to the dance the other night.

Francis wondered when the last time had been that she cared what a man thought about what she wore. She'd never asked Sam, and she couldn't remember him ever remarking on anything she wore. Except for her old bathrobe, and that was only because it annoyed him.

Thinking of her evening gown reminded her that she did have pieces of that outfit left. If she put on the ivory lingerie she'd gotten to wear with that sequined ruby dress, she'd at least feel desirable. The ruby dress was little more than threads in her closet now, but the accessories were still good.

Finally, she settled on wearing the navy suit skirt and a light blue silk blouse with a pearl necklace.

By the time Francis slipped her feet into the strappy high heels she'd also purchased to wear with the sequined dress and ran a mauve lipstick over her lips, she decided she could at least compete with women like this Rose person who apparently visited Flint in his dreams.

"Coat?" Flint held up a parka jacket for Francis almost as soon as she came into the kitchen.

Something about Francis was different, and Flint didn't like the hungry look he'd surprised in Sam's eyes. The other man might look like he was all starch and collar, but Flint guessed he wasn't as comfortable with Francis as he looked. And who could blame him? Francis had a softness about her face that would make any man want to explore her further.

"So soon?"

Flint nodded. "I want us to be all set in the church before the regulars start to come in."

"I'll see you after the service," Sam said a little grimly to Francis as he looked at Flint.

Flint nodded. Sam hadn't been too happy about the arrangements, but Flint had insisted. There was only a remote possibility of trouble, but he didn't want to have to worry about Sam if anything did happen.

Everything looked white and gray when Francis

stepped out of the house. She had accepted the parka from Flint and had wrapped a wool scarf around her neck, as well. It was hard to be a fashion plate in the middle of a Montana winter. The air was so cold her breath made short white puffs, and she pulled her scarf up so that it covered her chin. White snow lay softly over the yard outside the house. A few dog prints and the prints Flint had made when he went out earlier to warm up the pickup were all that disturbed the soft white blanket.

"Garth said we got another four inches last night," Flint noted as he opened Francis's door on the four-wheel-drive pickup. At the same time, he looked in the back of the pickup to check that the usual winter shovel hadn't been taken out to be used on some farm chore. It hadn't. "The roads will be rough."

"Maybe some of it will melt off by the time we come home from church," Francis said as she climbed into the pickup cab. She'd needed to take her high heels off and put snow boots on, but she carried the shoes in her hands. She's slip them on when she got to church just like most of the other women would do. "Might all melt."

"Not likely." Flint had already become accustomed to the Montana cold. When it snowed, the air was heavy. But the rest of the time, the air was light and brittle.

Flint opened and closed his own door quickly.

The heater was working, and the air inside the pickup cab was slightly warmer than that outside.

Flint removed his gloves and turned the heater to defrost. The windows were fogged over, but the defroster was already clearing small circles on them. He breathed in deeply. He could smell the fragrance of peaches coming from Francis. "Nice perfume."

"It's just lotion."

Sylvia had lent her the lotion when she had heard Francis and Flint were going to attend church together.

Francis smiled to remember the other woman standing with the bottle of lotion in her hand.

"But it's not a date," Francis had protested halfheartedly as the other woman flipped open the cap to the lotion and tipped it toward Francis's hands. "It's just church."

Sylvia had smiled and squeezed some lotion into Francis's outstretched hands. "You're going to a church, not a convent. Lots of romances start there."

Francis had smoothed the lotion into her hands and arms and now, talking to Flint, she was glad she had. "Winter is always hard on the skin."

Flint shifted from park into reverse and looked in the rearview mirror.

"It's the cold moisture in the air," Francis muttered as she watched Flint back the pickup away from the ranch house. He'd shaved since last night. His skin was smooth, and the lines of his face were more pronounced than when he had a little stubble. He'd put a suit jacket over his shoulder holster, and his gun blended into the contours of his chest so that it wasn't noticeable. His head was turned so that he could look back while he steered the pickup past a snowdrift. Francis had never noticed what a strong neck he had. Of course, when she'd known him, he'd been a young man of twenty. His neck had had plenty of years to change since then. They'd both changed in those years.

"And the wind," Francis continued. "It's been windy for the past few months. Must be El Niño or the drought or something,"

Flint had turned the pickup around, and he was heading down the gravel road that ran down Garth's property to the main county road. The road was bumpy. The November rains had filled the road with ruts. Those ruts had frozen solid in December and stayed that way.

"The drought makes it hard for the ranchers around here," Flint said. He had listened to the ranch hands at Garth's place. The men talked about the weather first thing in the morning and the last thing at night. Last summer had been dry, and although the winter had been cold, the snowfall in the mountains had been below normal.

"Some of them are on the verge of selling out," Francis said. "One more dry summer could do them in. The cost of feed gets too high, and they can't afford to run as many cattle.''

Flint grunted in sympathy. "They need to diversify. Ranch part time and then do something else.''

"Don't think they haven't tried to do that,'' Francis said. "But there's no business around here. Only three or four jobs—the post office, the job Matthew does at the hardware store, and then the café—but Linda and Duane run that.''

"It'd be a pity for anyone to leave,'' Flint said. The morning sun was fading from red to pink as it inched its way up the sky. When he looked to his right, he saw the foothills of the Big Sheep Mountain Range covered in a thick collar of snow. Snow hadn't collected on the sides of the mountains, and they were a gray-brown. "It's a beautiful, restful place to be.''

Flint was surprised at the sentiment he felt. He thought he'd grown more callused than that over the years. A home was only a place to hang one's hat. He would have bet he'd learned that lesson. Any land was the same as any other. Each plot of dirt the same as any other plot.

"Everyone has been thinking of business ideas,'' Francis said. "From dude ranches to quilting factories. Even jelly making—Mrs. Hargrove said folks might pay for some of the homemade jelly folks around here make.''

"I still can't believe everyone around here makes

jelly," Flint said incredulously. "What century is this, anyway?"

Francis only smiled. "We've lived through long, hard winters in Dry Creek. Makes us appreciate home-canned jellies and fruit. Nothing tastes better when the snow is deep than something you've grown yourself. Brings back the smell of summer."

For the first time, Flint began to think about those five acres his grandmother had left him in her will. He hadn't given them any attention for years. Maybe now, before he left, he should plant something. He didn't need to plant fruits or vegetables on them, but some kind of plant would be nice. Maybe some rosebushes would do well down by the trickle of a creek that ran through his grandmother's land during the spring months when the snow ran off the mountains. Wild roses might grow without extra water. Or a tree. A tree would surely grow. He suddenly realized he'd never planted anything anywhere before.

The sun had lost its pink and was a thin bright yellow that hovered over the day.

The pickup cab was warm enough, and Flint turned the defroster off. The steering on the four-wheel drive was stiff and required all of Flint's attention. Still, it was cozy inside the cab as he and Francis bumped along the county road. On each side of the narrow country road were wide ditches that caught the snow. Beside each ditch was a fence running along the road, dividing the grassland. The road rose and then dipped along with the low, rolling countryside.

"Robert moved his plane," Flint noticed. The small plane had been parked beside that far fence for the past three days. Now a thin path made by the plane wheels ran through the snow. "Must be desperate if he's thinking of taking off in this kind of snow."

"I hear the café needed supplies and he was having some airlifted in. I think they're just dropping the supplies by the old plane. That's why he moved it—so the drop would go smooth."

"Must be nice to be rich."

Francis smiled. "I hear he's bringing in crates of frozen asparagus and caviar. His mother is determined to bring the finer foods to Dry Creek for the kids. It's almost a cross-cultural experience for most of them to tackle something like caviar."

"They can live full lives without caviar," Flint said.

Francis shrugged. "It doesn't hurt them to try new things."

Garth's ranch buildings were behind them as they drove, and Flint saw another ranch off to the left in the distance. The house and outbuildings were sheltered by a small grove of trees, their branches leafless and stark on a winter day. Someone had planted those trees in some past hopeful time.

Flint was looking for the low-lying outline of a small plane, but instead he saw something else low on the horizon. He could see a horse and rider from a distance coming down the road.

Now what is some fool doing out with a horse on a morning like this? Flint thought, forgetting that it had not been that many mornings ago when that rider would have been him.

Chapter Ten

The horse grew more familiar as Flint drove closer to it. Finally, he even recognized the man riding the horse.

What had possessed that old man to strike out on horseback with the snow from last night's blizzard still fresh on the ground? If the old man didn't care what happened to himself, he should at least be more considerate of Honey.

The last Flint had seen Honey she'd been cozy in the old chicken coop on his grandmother's place. He'd made arrangements for Duane Edison to bring her back to the café and keep her in the shed behind the place. Flint planned to visit Honey there after church and take her a few of the apples he'd gotten from Mrs. Hargrove. He'd discovered the horse had a fondness for them.

The ruts in the road were deeper, and Flint needed to slow down as he came closer to the old man. The pickup wasn't going more than five miles an hour. The old man crossed the road so that he would be riding past the passenger side of the pickup.

"What's he up to?" Flint asked.

Francis started to roll down her window. "Must be rabbit hunting. He's got his rifle with him. Mr. Gossett," Francis called cheerfully. "Good morning."

The old man was still in front of the pickup when he stopped riding.

A warning prickle ran down Flint's spine. Something about the determined set of the old man's shoulders made him uneasy. "Don't open the door. And roll that window back up."

Francis turned to him in disbelief. "You're going to leave him here?"

"Yes."

"But he's an old man and it's freezing out there," Francis protested. "Look at him. He might even be senile. Wandering around without a scarf on his head. He'll catch pneumonia."

Flint hesitated. He didn't want Francis to think he was heartless. The old man did look almost senile. Maybe Flint's spine had known too many bad men over the years so that he couldn't tell the bad from the simpleminded. Still. "I didn't tell him to saddle up and play cowboy on a morning like this."

"But he's on Honey," Francis added as though she and the horse were now fast friends. "You know she isn't enjoying this romp through the snow. Look at her. She looks hungry."

"She's had plenty of oats. She just wants one of those apples I have in the back of the pickup."

Francis looked through the cab window to the bed of the pickup. There they were—a dozen apples tied in a red mesh bag.

"Tell him I'll send someone back for him," Flint said to Francis as he pulled closer to the old man. "But then roll up that window. We can't be too careful."

"You suspect Mr. Gossett?" Francis asked in surprise as she eyed the old man through the windshield dubiously. "Surely he's harmless. I wouldn't think he'd be—you know—"

"Bright enough?"

Francis nodded. "And he doesn't know anyone but a few people in Dry Creek. Never has any visitors or anything. No friends. No family."

"A man doesn't need friends to commit a crime. Nor does he need to be particularly intelligent."

Francis began rolling down the pickup window again. The crank was stiff and she bent her head as she moved it. She stopped when the window was a third of the way down and called to the old man who was just a little ahead of the slow-moving pickup. "Don't worry. We'll send someone back for you. And you should have a scarf in weather like this. Is there one in your pockets?''

The old man scowled. The woman in the pickup sounded like his mother. Scolding him for forgetting something like he was a little kid.

He'd show her who was a little kid, the old man thought in satisfaction.

''I don't need a scarf,'' the old man said as he took the barrel of his rifle and slapped it against the rump of the horse so that she nervously jumped into the middle of the road and reared up.

Flint swore as he pushed his foot hard into the brake pedal. Honey was practically on top of the pickup hood when she reared up like that. ''What in blazes?''

The pickup stopped, and Flint instinctively put his right hand out to push Francis down in the seat.

''What—'' Francis resisted the shove, more out of bewilderment than anything else.

But it was enough. The time he'd taken to try to shield her behind the metal of the pickup cost him. He should have gone for his gun first, he told himself later. By the time he brought his hand to his holster the harmless old man had swung his rabbit-hunting rifle around and had drawn a bead on Francis.

''Easy now,'' Flint murmured. Francis was staring at the rifle. ''Don't move.''

"Throw the gun out of there." The old man sat on the horse and yelled.

Flint put his hands up in plain view. Next time, he'd trust his spine. "Let me step out first."

The first thing Flint needed to do was to put some distance between himself and Francis. Guns went with guns, and he'd bet the old man would swing the barrel of that old rifle around to follow him if he stepped outside the pickup. At least then, if there were any bullets fired, Francis would have a chance. An old rifle like that probably wouldn't hold more than one bullet. If Flint could get the man to fire at him, Francis would be safe.

The old man snorted and steadied his gun. "I ain't that stupid. You've got to the count of three."

Francis was frozen. She told herself she should know what to do. She'd taken a hostage negotiation class at work. She was supposed to know what to do. But her mind was blank.

"One." The old man called out the number with a certain amount of satisfaction.

"I'm putting it out now," Flint said as he slowly moved his hand toward the holster. The defroster had been off long enough that the windshield on the pickup had a thin film coating it. In another five minutes, the view would be fuzzy from where the old man sat on the horse. But Flint didn't have five minutes. "I'll need to open the door to throw it."

"Stick it through the window," the old man ordered.

So much for that idea, Flint thought. He'd considered opening the door and swinging down to shoot at the old man from there. He'd be far enough away from Francis that the bullet from the man's rifle wouldn't be coming in her direction.

Francis was cold. She could feel her teeth start to chatter.

Flint could hear her teeth start to chatter. He didn't dare look at Francis, though. He kept his eyes on the old man.

"Two." The old man counted loudly.

Flint touched the butt of his gun as he unsnapped his shoulder holster smoothly. "Take it easy. It's coming."

"Handle first," the old man instructed.

Flint drew the gun out with the fingertips of one hand. "No problem."

Flint squeezed the barrel of his gun as he swung it around to the side of the pickup. The cold made the gun slippery, and he had to hold it tight.

"I need to roll my window down."

The old man shook his head slightly. "Push it through the other window by Francis."

Flint didn't like reaching across Francis with his gun. It would keep the eyes of the old man focused on her. But Flint didn't hesitate. He reached over to the few inches of open space in Francis's window.

The gun slipped over the side and clanked against the side of the pickup on the way down.

The old man lowered his rifle a little. Not much, but enough so that Flint began to breathe again.

"It's not too late to let us go, you know," Flint called out the window to the old man. "Whatever it is that's bothering you—we can talk about it."

"Ain't nothing bothering me," the old man said. "I just need to get out of here."

"Well, why didn't you say so?" Flint forced his voice to relax. The safe period in any hostage situation was the setting of the terms. "I'd be happy to take you someplace. Just put the gun down and we'll see that you get where you need to go."

The old man slid off the back of the horse right next to the pickup. The barrel of his rifle wavered, but Flint didn't make any sudden moves. A gun in the hands of an amateur was always a potentially deadly thing. It was too easy to underestimate someone.

"I'm sure the boys in the bunkhouse have something to drink, as well," Francis offered quietly. "Whiskey, for sure. Maybe some Scotch. I'm sure you'd like a little drink for the road."

"Don't have time for a drink," the old man said as he reached out and opened the door beside Francis. "Move over. I'm coming in."

The old man grabbed the inside back of the cab and started to pull himself in. He must have remembered Flint's gun, and bent down to pick it up from the ground.

"If you want me to drive you somewhere— maybe Miles City—I'd be happy to," Flint said calmly, not commenting on the other gun. He was afraid of this. His own gun made the man's rabbit rifle look as harmless as a water pistol. "But we don't need Francis to come along. Why don't you let her get out and ride the horse back to her brother's ranch."

"I'm not stupid," Mr. Gossett snapped as he shoved himself into the cab and slammed the door behind him.

"No one ever said you were," Flint murmured soothingly.

The heat inside the cab was beginning to warm the old man's clothes, and they were starting to smell.

The old man eyed Flint and Francis. "Nobody's leaving here, and you'll drive me where I tell you— but it won't be Miles City. The road past Dry Creek is closed. I heard Highway 89 is blocked off until the snowplows get through. Don't think a pickup will get through."

"Maybe your best bet is the horse, then," Flint said. *Sorry, Honey,* he thought ruefully. *You take him away, and I'll come get you both—and I'll bring you some of those apples you like. And not just the*

*small bunch I have in the back of the pickup. I'll
shake down a whole tree for you.*

The old man snorted. "Couldn't pay me to get
back on that animal—she's practically worthless.
Stubborn as a mule. Almost had me setting out on
foot a time or two."

Flint smiled inside. He could always count on
Honey.

"If no one can drive you and the horse won't take
you," Francis said, "then you need to decide
whether it is really important that you go. If it's
groceries you need—or something more substantial
to drink than tea—or anything else—"

"What I need is to get out of the state!"

"Then you'll need to wait," Francis said calmly.
She had hoped he was just a fool in search of al-
cohol. The alternatives were not as pleasant.
"There's no way to go today."

"There's the plane—the plane that flew in to
bring the lobsters for the party," the old man said
with satisfaction in his voice. "The plane that that
millionaire fellow owns. That's where I want you to
take me."

"I don't know where the plane is." Flint stalled.
"He might have even flown it out of here."

"Just follow them tracks," the old man said as
though that settled the matter. "I was starting to
follow them when I spotted you. Decided no point
in riding on that old horse. Especially when you've
got a warm pickup that'll get us there just as good."

Flint looked over to see the wide tracks of the plane that ran on the other side of the fence. Why couldn't Robert Buckwalter have driven his plane deeper into the pasture instead of along the fence?

The old man nodded. "You can go now."

The roads were frozen, bumpy, and Flint needed both hands to control the steering on the pickup. But he still curved his shoulder slightly away from the seat so that Francis could nestle close to him. Francis sat with her legs on the driver's side of the stick shift. Flint knew her decision to be so close to him was made because she wanted to be as far away as possible from the old man, but he welcomed her presence anyway. It felt right to have her sandwiched in next to him.

Francis watched Flint's hands on the steering wheel. He'd taken off his gloves so that he could grip the wheel more securely, and the cold made the skin on his hands whiter than usual. They were strong hands, the fingers big and agile.

She had a sudden recollection of the last time they'd sat this close in a pickup.

"Whatever happened to that old pickup of yours?" Francis asked softly.

The old man hadn't said anything since he climbed into the pickup. He'd just sat there with one hand holding Flint's gun and the other steadying the rifle against his leg closest to the door. Francis tried to pretend he wasn't there.

"My grandmother finally sold it to some other kid." Flint smiled. Until he'd met Francis, he'd poured his heart into that old pickup. "Wonder if he ever got our initials off the door."

Francis smiled. She had forgotten about the initials Flint had painted on the door. Two swirling black *F*s with lots of extra curlicues.

"He did." The old man surprised them both by speaking. "Jim Jett bought it—painted it black all over. That took care of the initials."

"I don't suppose there's much in Dry Creek you don't know," Flint began tentatively. He wondered how the man would respond to flattery. "You being a pillar of the community and all."

The old man snorted. "You know I ain't no pillar of nothing."

"Well, your father was," Flint continued the conversation and prayed the old man had liked his father. "I heard what he did in the big drought—getting people to stay and make a town. He was a real hero in these parts."

"He was a fool. He should have left Dry Creek when he had a chance. The whole town never amounted to anything. And my father—all he ever had to his name was his few acres in Dry Creek, Montana."

"He had friends," Francis added softly. "And the respect of his neighbors."

"It took me two years to save up enough money to buy a decent headstone for his grave," the old man muttered bitterly. "After that, I figured why bother."

"But you never left the area?" Flint asked softly.

"Where would I go?"

For a blinding moment Flint envied the old man his certainty about where he belonged in his life. Love it or hate it, Dry Creek was the old man's home. Flint had bounced around for years, never feeling connected to any place.

The old man pointed out the window. "There's the plane."

Flint could just make out the dark shape against the white snow ahead. No, wait. There was more than one black shape.

"There's another pickup there," Francis said, her voice neutral. Her mind was busy calculating the odds. Another pickup could be a problem or it could be a solution. She wondered which Flint thought it would be.

There was a time when she would have known what he thought. Would have comfortably finished his sentences for him when he talked. At the time, she had thought it was because they were so much in love. Now she wondered. They had been young and foolish. The fact that they had run off to Las Vegas without planning enough to even have luggage with them showed just how foolish.

"You'll stay in the pickup when we get there," Flint ordered Francis as he drove closer. He didn't like the fact that the old man was holding Flint's gun closer now. That gun had altogether too many bullets in it waiting to be fired.

"I'll say who stays where," the old man protested heatedly.

"She stays in the pickup." Flint ignored his words.

The old man grunted.

"Maybe we should all stay—just turn around and go where we need to go in the pickup," Francis offered. She didn't like the thought of Flint being alone with the crazy old man. "The roads might be open. You know those weather people—they're always behind the times. Maybe the roads have been cleared by now. We could drive to the main road and find out."

Francis's leg had pressed itself against Flint. And her scent—she smelled of summer peaches. He didn't dare turn and look fully at her because he didn't want the old man to get nervous.

Besides, Flint didn't really need to see her to know what she looked like. He had memorized her face over twenty years ago and he could still pull the picture out of his mind. Her eyes were the color of the earth after the first fall frost, full of brown shadows and dark green highlights with shimmer that promised depths unknown. Her eyes were usually somber. He had loved to tease her just to watch that moment when her eyes would turn from serious to playful indignation.

Flint moved his hand to the knob of the gearshift

even though he had no further gears left and wouldn't be shifting down. He just wanted to rest his hand closer to her.

Francis had never been more aware of Flint than she was at that moment. Maybe it was because of the danger around them. Maybe it was because of the long years she'd spent missing him.

Whatever it was, she had to slip her hand under her leg so that it wouldn't reach out and caress Flint's wrist. His arm was covered with the sleeve of a bulky winter jacket. His hands had been without gloves long enough now that they would be cold. But his wrist was the meeting place between cold and warm.

The pickup was bumping along closer to the plane. Without the four-wheel drive, the vehicle would have been stuck in at least a dozen different snowdrifts since they'd started following the plane tracks.

Flint had considered letting the pickup accidentally get stuck, but he didn't want to annoy the old man. Especially since staging a delay wasn't the best way to stop Mr. Gossett. Fifty years of progress would take care of that. Flint was confident the old man would take one look at the sophisticated instrument panel on the plane and give up any hope of flying it out of here. Even if the old man had flown a plane once in his youth, he would be bewildered today.

The fact that someone else was at the plane com-

plicated things. Flint suspected it was Robert Buckwalter who had come out to the plane. If it was, the
old man had a pilot. That would change the odds on
everything.

Francis sensed Flint's worry. Nothing in his face
had changed since they spotted that pickup, but she
gradually sensed the tension in him. *We're really in
danger,* she realized numbly. *Dear God,* The
thought came to her almost unbidden. *We need help.*

Francis was tired of worrying about the problems
between her and Flint. Just like she instinctively
turned to God when she needed help, she also
wanted to turn to Flint. They were in trouble, and
she didn't want to face it alone. She slipped her hand
from under her leg and brought it up to lightly touch
Flint's wrist.

Flint's hand responded immediately. It moved off
the gearshift and enclosed her hand.

I am home, Francis thought. His hand was cold.
Ice cold. But it didn't matter. His hand could rival
the temperature of the Arctic Circle and she'd want
to hold it. She could face anything if they were together hand in hand.

Chapter Eleven

If a person didn't know better, this could be a view on a postcard, Francis mused.

The morning sun was bright on the snow-covered hills leading up to the Big Sheep Mountain Range. The mountains themselves were low and didn't have any of the peaks that were found in other mountain ranges in Montana.

There were no houses on the horizon and no trees. Usually there were no signs of civilization up here except the thin lines of barbed-wire fence that divided the various sections of land that had belonged to her father and now belonged to her brother, Garth. Some of the land would be planted in wheat this coming spring. Some of it would be left for free-range grazing. Right now, it was empty. All of the cattle had been brought closer to the main house because of the storm.

The only mar in the otherwise peaceful picture was the tracks in the snow. There were now two sets of tracks. One set was partially filled in with drifting snow. The other set of tracks was newer. Both led to the small twin-engine plane that was parked next to one of the barbed-wire fences that followed the country road. Past the plane was a piece of land that had been scraped clean of snow. Either a snowplow had done it or it had been shoveled clean by hand.

"It must be Robert," Flint said softly. There was no one standing outside in the area between the plane and the Jeep, but it must be Robert. Who else would care enough about an airstrip to make one on a day like this?

Flint felt a twist in his stomach. With an airstrip and a pilot, there would be no stopping the old man from flying.

That's what Flint had been afraid of— He didn't want the old man airborne. Not that he knew for sure they would all be safer if old man Gossett had no hope of getting that plane in the air. But gunfire was much more likely if the old man even thought he could get them in the air.

"I'll do the talking," Mr. Gossett announced suddenly. "Don't want you two scaring them off."

Flint stopped the pickup as far away from the plane as he felt he could. Whoever had driven the

Jeep in here must be inside the plane. "They haven't got any place to go, anyway."

The old man renewed his grip on the two guns he held. "This won't take long."

"You'll want to be careful with that gun of mine," Flint said softly. "It's federal property. Use it to commit a crime and they'll lock you up and throw away the key."

The old man looked confused.

"You've seen the notices in the post office." Flint kept talking. The old man was of the era that could be intimidated by the government—maybe. "You'd do best to just leave it on the ground. Besides," Flint added for good measure, "that rifle of yours looks like it has seen some action. Don't think you'd need any more persuasion than she can give you."

The old man looked proud as he gripped the gun tighter. "She's a good shooter, all right."

There was a large tarp—no, it was a parachute, Francis realized—as well as ten, maybe twelve boxes sitting next to the plane. The parachute was white, and a dozen ropes swirled around it on the ground. On the other side of the parachute the four-wheel-drive Jeep was parked. Deep boot prints were all around the boxes and led up to the plane.

"That's the Edisons' Jeep," the old man said thoughtfully as he peered out the windshield. "Wonder if it's their boy, Duane, out there."

Flint prayed it would be. He thought the old man might have a harder time hurting someone from Dry Creek than he would a stranger. Sort of a you-never-hurt-the-ones-you-know theory.

"I heard Robert Buckwalter was having some more supplies flown in for the café—with all the kids around these days they are running low on everything." Francis spoke nervously.

Mr. Gossett shook his head in disgust. "In my day, you wouldn't find anyone flying in supplies. We'd eat bread and beans if that's all that was available. Kids today are too soft."

Flint believed in diversionary tactics. He agreed heartily. "You can say that again. Most of them aren't worth their salt."

Francis felt the faint squeeze Flint gave her fingers. She understood his message.

"They should all be sent to reform school," Francis agreed. "Teach them some manners."

The old man nodded thoughtfully. "They wouldn't like it—locked in with everyone else. I know I wouldn't."

"We could meet with the authorities about this," Flint offered. He had his fingers crossed that the old man would take the bait. "They'll understand how you feel about being locked up. I'll drive you back to the café and we can make a call. If you turn state's evidence on this rustling business, you might get off with probation. I'll see to it that you meet with the right people—maybe even the state governor—or a congressman.''

The old man snorted. ''Worthless politicians. I'd rather deal with them kids any day.''

''The press then.'' Flint continued the bribe. ''Say you don't confess to anything. We could get the press out here and do an article for the Billings paper. You'd be famous.''

The old man paled. Then he raised Flint's gun and jerked it at him. ''Who in blazes wants to be famous? I just want to be left alone.''

Well, that eliminated most of the mental-illness categories, Flint thought in resignation. He didn't know whether it would be easier to deal with someone who was crazy or someone who was stone-cold sane and just mean.

''You call out and let them know we're here.'' The old man jerked his head toward the plane. ''They'll come out at the sound of your voice. Be friendly-like.''

Flint hoped Mr. Gossett was wrong and that whoever was inside the plane would stay right there.

''Anybody home?'' Flint rolled down his window and called out. ''You've got company. Company and trouble—they come together—''

''Hush,'' the old man hissed.

Francis felt the sweep of frigid air coming in the open window. She wanted to snuggle closer to Flint, but she felt the tension in his body and did not want to be in the way if he needed to move fast.

Flint's heart sank. He saw a figure standing in the open door to the small plane. His hint had gone unheard.

"It's the chef," Flint murmured. Another figure joined the first. "And Robert."

"Let's go meet them," Mr. Gossett ordered Flint as he grabbed the door handle. "I've got plans."

Flint hoped he never heard the words "I've got plans" again. Mr. Gossett kept waving the guns around, and his plans were soon implemented. Robert Buckwalter was able to assess the situation quickly. Flint would wager the other man had had his own share of training in how to deal with hostage situations. Since Robert traveled internationally, he might even have some training on terrorist activities.

It only took a minute for Robert Buckwalter to assure the old man that he would fly him anywhere he could.

"The plane's only got enough fuel to fly to someplace like Fargo, North Dakota—or we could head for Billings if you want to stay in Montana," Robert explained to the older man just like he was a pilot planning a routine flight.

"I'll take Fargo. Let's all get in."

Robert nodded toward the old man and eyed him speculatively. "The fuel will last longer if the plane is lighter. I'd say you're about one hundred seventy pounds?''

The old man nodded.

"I'll go with you to fly this thing, but you don't want to take the others—it's unnecessary weight."

"I'll need a hostage."

Flint stepped forward. "That would be me."

The old man snorted. "I don't think so. I'll take her." He jerked his head at the young woman who was standing by Buckwalter's side. "She's a skinny little thing. Can't weigh much."

"It's not just about weight," Flint said. He kept moving around, hoping to find a moment when the old man was off guard. But Mr. Gossett kept his gun trained on one of the women at all times. "I can talk to the authorities for you."

"You speak English?" He barked the words at the chef.

She nodded.

"She can talk for me," the old man insisted. "Now, you two men get all the boxes out of that plane. I don't want any unnecessary weight holding us back."

Francis shivered. She and Jenny, the chef who worked for Mrs. Buckwalter, were standing together near the door to the plane. Mr. Gossett stood nearby and held Flint's gun loosely in his hand.

"You'll be all right," Francis whispered to the young woman. "Flint will get help."

The young woman nodded mutely.

Francis prayed she was right. Once the plane was airborne she and Flint could drive one of the pickups the ten or so miles back to Dry Creek and get help sent ahead. If they could alert the airports in Fargo and Billings, they should be able to stop the old man without anyone getting hurt.

"Now, everyone out of the plane," the old man ordered.

All the boxes had been thrown to the ground. Flint and Robert jumped to the ground from the open door of the plane.

Flint had his plan. The floor of the plane was about four feet up from the ground. There would be no way the old man could climb into the plane and hold onto both guns at the same time. That would be when Flint would tackle him.

"Now—you two—get down on the ground." The old man jerked his gun at Francis and Flint.

"What?" Flint bit back a further protest. This was a twist he hadn't counted on.

"But it's cold." Robert stepped in. "Let them at least go sit in the pickup—or even the Jeep."

"The ground. Now," the old man ordered, his voice rising in agitation. "I don't have all day, I gotta get out of here."

Francis lowered herself to the ground. The snow was not yet packed, and it was like sinking into a down pillow. An icy cold down pillow. She sat down with her legs crossed in front of her.

"You, too," the old man said curtly as he glanced over at Flint. "I want you with your back to her—" the old man shifted his gaze to Jenny "—and you get some rope from those boxes to tie them up."

"You're not going to leave them like that?" Jenny protested. "It's freezing out here. They'll—" Jenny swallowed and didn't finish her sentence.

Francis could finish it for her. If she and Flint were tied and left in a snowdrift like this, they could die.

"What does it matter to me if they get cold?" the old man demanded. "That'll teach them to come snooping around, asking questions. Butting into a man's private life."

Flint watched the old man and didn't like what he saw. Maybe it wasn't a choice of whether the old man was crazy or a criminal—maybe he was both.

"It's a federal offense to kill an FBI agent," Flint said softly as he moved to step between Francis and the old man.

"Not if it's an act of God," the old man said with a humorless chuckle as he shifted to adjust for Flint's move.

Unless Flint wanted to anger the old man, he knew he shouldn't move again right away. Once step could be casual. Two would be a threat.

"But surely you're not planning—" Robert

Buckwalter protested in disbelief from where he stood beside the plane.

"I'm not debating this," the old man said firmly, still keeping his gun bead steady on Francis at all times. "I suggest everyone just do what they're told."

Francis had kept her head down for this entire conversation. Flint wondered if she were praying and then decided he hoped she was. Maybe God would listen to someone like Francis. She sure didn't deserve to be out here in the middle of a snowdrift with a crazy man threatening to shoot her.

"Why should we do anything you say?" Francis looked up, and her chin came up defiantly. "You're going to leave us tied up here no matter what we do. You can't bring yourself to shoot us. But you'll let us freeze to death. From where I sit, there's not much else you can do to us."

Flint cringed when he heard what Francis said. The old man was unstable at best. Defiance wasn't a good choice.

For the next ten minutes, Francis tried to take her words back. She kept saying "I'm sorry" like it was a mantra. It hadn't mattered. The old man hadn't been listening.

She kept apologizing until the small plane moved down the makeshift airstrip and took off.

"It's okay, it'll be okay," Flint said behind her

back, and Francis realized he had been saying the words softly for some time now.

Francis stopped apologizing to the old man who wasn't even there any longer. She was so numb she no longer shivered. The old man had shown what else he could do. First he'd taken Flint's jacket, then hers. He'd thrown the coats in the back of the plane. Then he'd forced her to remove her dress and Flint to remove his suit. Those, too, had gone into the back of the plane.

"Just to show you what a good guy I am, I'm leaving you your underwear." Mr. Gossett grinned. "Wouldn't want the proper ladies of Dry Creek to get in a tizzy when someone finds the bodies."

The old man laughed then instructed Jenny, "Tie 'em tight. Don't want either of them wandering around out here and getting lost."

Flint wanted to shout at the old man, to call him names. The strength of the desire shook him. He was losing his edge. It was unprofessional. He knew that. It wasn't by the book. It wasn't smart. *But it's Francis,* his mind screamed.

Flint forced himself to focus. He needed all of his energy just to keep himself and Francis alive.

Before the old man climbed into the plane, he took Jenny with him and walked to both vehicles. The Jeep's hood was stiff, but he had made Jenny open it and then he had reached in and pulled out a handful of spark plugs and stuffed them in his pocket. He had done the same with the pickup that Flint and Francis had driven.

It was at that point that Francis had broken down and started apologizing more loudly. She was still whimpering, the words coming softly from her lips.

Flint tried to move his arms so that he could turn around and hold Francis. He was terrified. The freezing cold was a worse enemy than any he had faced. At least, with a kidnapper or a terrorist, you had the chance of talking them out of their plans. But the cold? What did the weather care for either threats or emotions?

Finally, Flint moved so that his hands could grip Francis's. The plane was growing smaller in the mid-morning sky. It had started east and then slowly turned to head west. The old man must have changed his mind and settled on Billings, after all.

Flint murmured again, "It'll be okay."

Francis hiccuped and then quieted. Her throat was beginning to hurt from the gulps of cold air that she had breathed. Every exposed inch of skin on her body was tingling. She felt like she was being pricked with a thousand daggers. She forced herself to focus. She was facing her death, and only a few things were still important.

"I should say I'm sorry," Francis said calmly. The only warm place on her body was her hand, and that was because Flint held it in his. "I should have waited for you twenty years ago instead of thinking you had deserted me. I should have trusted you."

"I should have trusted you, too," Flint said as he strained against the ropes tying them together so he could move his back closer to hers. Finally, their bare shoulder blades met. Francis leaned into him, and he could feel the elastic ridge of her bra strap. Their skins gradually warmed.

Flint continued to strain at the ropes. The old man had watched Jenny carefully as she knotted the ropes, but Flint believed she would have left them room to escape if there was any way she could.

"I wish we'd gotten to church this morning," Francis continued pensively. "I was thinking of going back, you know—not that I guess I was ever there much as an adult. But still, there's a sense of going back. Looking for the hope I'd lost."

"I know what you mean."

"It would be a comfort to know how to pray to God."

"My grandmother always said you just open your mouth and talk to Him."

"Still, it would have been nice to pray in a church," Francis continued, her voice drifting. "Do you suppose they'll come looking for us when we don't show up this morning?"

"Sure," Flint lied. He'd already thought of that. He and Francis had left early. No one would miss them for a half hour. By then the service would just be starting, and they would think that Francis was taking longer to get dressed or that they had gotten stuck in a snowdrift or changed their minds altogether. It would be a good hour before they would even start to worry.

Flint knew it would be several hours more before anyone would find them. And that would be too long for people left in a snowbank in ten-below-zero weather without even a shirt between them.

"But if they don't come right away we could make some kind of shelter from those boxes," Flint said brightly. He had no idea if a box house would keep them alive long enough. What he did know is that Francis needed hope. He needed it himself.

"And there might be something to start a fire with in those boxes," Francis agreed willingly. "Some cooking utensil or something. Chefs are always flambéing something or another."

Flint felt the ropes at his wrist start to give.

"Twist your hand away from me," Flint instructed. "I think I've got it."

One of Flint's hands scraped through the knot. He pulled his hand up and flexed his fingers. The cold was stiffening them more quickly than he had thought. He needed to act fast.

"If we had a fire, we might be able to find something to burn that would make enough black smoke to make someone curious," Flint said as he twisted his other hand to free it as well.

Finally, both of Flint's hands were free.

He turned and saw Francis's back. Her shoulders were hunched, and the thin line of her spine stood out whiter than the rest of her skin. She had curled her hair for church, and the curls still bounced. Her hands were still behind her back, and with the extra room in the knots since Flint had removed his hands, she was twisting her hands to free them.

The threat of death does strange things to a man, Flint reflected. It certainly made him dare things he wouldn't otherwise.

"Come." Flint turned Francis and drew her to him.

Francis knew that their only victory might be untying their hands. She knew they might not have a way to burn the boxes for heat and that they might freeze to death after all. But she would still be glad that they had freed their hands and could hug one another.

Flint's chest had changed since they used to embrace. He'd been a lanky young man, and his chest used to be wiry. Now his chest was solid. Muscles rippled as his arms tightened around her.

Flint almost couldn't breathe, and he wasn't so sure it was because of the biting cold in his lungs. He had Francis in his arms once again. He wanted to let his words of love spill out and cover them, but he didn't.

"I'll get us out of here," he said gruffly as he

pulled away from her. "If it's the last thing I do, I'll get us out of here."

Francis nodded. She was too cold to think.

Dear Lord, she thought, *we might actually die out here.* This time the thought did not terrify her.

"But if not, you'll hold me some more, won't you?" Francis asked quietly. "I mean, if it turns out that there's no hope? I don't want to die alone."

"You're not going to die," Flint promised fiercely as he forced himself to stand. The cold was beginning to slow him, too. "I'm going to look through those boxes that just came in. Then I'm going to see if the cigarette lighter in the Jeep works."

Flint stood and eyed the boxes. It was so cold the snow wasn't melting, and the boxes were not damp at all. He slowly counted ten large boxes. Quite a parachute drop. Nine of them had the red stamped logo of a supermarket on them. Howard's Gourmet Foods.

Flint was walking toward the first of those boxes when he noticed the tenth box in more detail. It was a rectangular box with the imprint of some clothing store on it.

"Bingo!" Flint shouted, and turned to Francis.

She was huddled in the snow where they'd been tied. Her skin was too white, and her eyes were half-closed. That was a bad sign.

"You need to move around," Flint urged her as

he quickly walked to her and held out his hand. "Come over here and let's open the boxes."

"I'm not sure I can," Francis said. But she took Flint's outstretched hand, and he slowly pulled her to her feet. Her body almost creaked as she moved.

"There's a clothing box." Flint led Francis over to where the boxes had been dumped. "Robert must have had them drop off some winter clothing along with the food."

"Maybe a—wool jacket—or thermal long johns," Francis whispered as Flint tore through the tape on the box. Her teeth were chattering in slow motion, and she needed to pause between words. "I do—hope—it's long johns."

"Well, it's—" Flint held up the first piece of clothing he pulled out and announced in disappointment "—a tuxedo."

The black jacket was made of silk. Even packed away as it had been, it was obviously expensive. Expensive and light enough for a summer evening.

Francis hugged herself and rubbed her arms slowly. She couldn't even feel her fingers.

"They must have come late," Francis said hoarsely. "The dance is already over."

Flint noticed that a small receipt was tucked into the box under the tuxedo jacket. He pulled it out. "I don't think it was meant for the dance—these are addressed to Laurel Blackstone."

"The woman who came in—the one who knew Robert Buckwalter?"

Flint nodded as he pulled out a pair of man's slacks. The black slacks had a shiny dark gray stripe down the leg. At least the slacks looked like they'd keep some of the cold away.

"My guess is she knew him rather well," Flint said as he pulled out the final garment in the box—a frothy wedding gown.

"My word," Francis breathed and then realized the implications of the dress. "Poor Jenny."

Francis had seen that the young chef was smitten with Robert Buckwalter. But it looked like Laurel Blackstone had expectations of her own.

The gown was beautiful. Francis reached out to touch the beaded flounces in the full skirt. Even in the bitter cold, she had to appreciate that gown. The bodice was made of soft ivory satin. A square-cut neckline was lined with satin trim and embedded pearls. Yards of sheer net fell from the waist and formed a train. "I've never seen anything so exquisite."

"Well, it's yours," Flint said as he handed the dress to her.

"But, I can't—"

"I suppose we could reverse them—but I don't think the dress would do nearly as much for me as it would for you," Flint joked.

"But it's Laurel's wedding dress," Francis protested. She might be in an extreme situation, but good manners should still mean something. "I can't just put on someone's dress and then—lie down and die in it."

Flint's heart gladdened at the pink consternation on Francis's face. She always was one to be concerned about the proper time and place of things. It was good to have her back. He'd been worried when she seemed so listless.

"Well, I guess that means I have to get into it then," Flint teased as he lifted the cloud of net over his head.

"Oh, don't be silly," Francis protested like he'd known she would. "Give me that thing."

"Gladly."

Flint couldn't restrain himself. He lifted the cloud of white net high and then, stepping forward, settled it over both Francis and himself. Inside the tangle, his lips found hers.

Francis felt Flint's warm breath seconds before she felt his lips on hers. She didn't bother to hide the purr that vibrated deep within her. A kiss, she decided, was a very nice thing.

Flint was adjusting his violet silk cummerbund and muttering about the fact that only a woman would buy a fancy cummerbund and no shirt when he heard a sound that made him turn and scan the horizon.

"Well, hallelujah! Look at that!"

Francis turned to look in the direction Flint was pointing. The dress was strangely warm for being so frothy. "What is that?"

Flint didn't need to see more of the distant figure to know in his gut that it was who he thought it was. "Honey!"

The horse neighed in response to Flint's call and started to trot toward them.

"Well, well," Flint said to himself. He was right about that horse. She made a fine partner.

"She came to get us?" Francis asked in gratitude.

"Close enough." Flint grinned as Honey did as he suspected she might and stopped at the back of his pickup to sniff the bag of apples he'd tossed there earlier. "Close enough."

Flint was careful to give Honey only half of the apples before handing the red mesh bag, half empty, to Francis. "Hold these."

Flint put his foot in the stirrup and swung himself into the saddle before reaching down and helping Francis climb up behind him.

Honey fidgeted for a moment, uncertain about the two adults on her back.

"Easy, girl." Flint soothed the horse as he smiled. The fidgeting made Francis lean in closer to him and clutch him fearfully around the middle.

Now this is how a hero is supposed to feel, Flint

said to himself in satisfaction as he recalled the last time he and Francis had been riding Honey.

"Let's go to town," Flint said softly to the horse. "We've got a bride to warm up."

Chapter Twelve

Heading down the country road into Dry Creek, Flint held Honey to a fast walk, at least most of the time. Now that he and Francis had some clothes on their backs, their heat loss was much less. He didn't want to risk Honey overexerting and becoming so cold she couldn't go on.

"What time is it?" Francis asked behind Flint's back. She'd recently lain her cheek against his tuxedo jacket for warmth, and he liked her nestling against his shoulder blades.

Flint lifted the back of his jacket so that Francis's arms would be covered as she clutched him. It left a draft on the middle of his back where the cummerbund ended, but it kept her arms warm, and she snuggled even closer to him.

"Ten to eleven," Flint said after looking down at

his sports watch. Mr. Gossett had apparently considered watches in the same necessary category as underwear and hadn't demanded that Flint take it off.

"Everyone will be at the church," Francis mumbled.

"That's what we want," Flint said. "We'll be able to mobilize everyone right away. The sheriff should be there still, and he can get in touch with the Billings police and any security they have at the airport."

"Do you think Jenny and Robert are all right?"

"Robert knows what he's doing." Flint comforted her as well as himself. "He won't take any unnecessary chances."

Flint didn't add that he was more worried about Jenny. He searched the skyline as though he might see the small plane. The young woman was high-spirited. High-spirited people tended to make themselves targets in hostage situations.

The morning seemed to warm a few degrees as the sun rose higher in the sky. It still wasn't warm enough to disturb the snow, however, and soft banks lined both sides of the country road they were riding down.

Honey seemed to sense they were close to Dry Creek and started to move faster as they took the last turn in the road before coming into the small cluster of buildings that made up Dry Creek.

Flint steered the horse toward the church. The

white frame building with its steep roof and empty
belfry had never looked so good to him. The double
doors at the top of the cement steps were closed, so
that must mean the service had started. If he remembered rightly, they kept the doors open in the summer during the services, and the hymns spilled out
into the area around the church. He had sometimes
sat on the last step and listened as a teenager. But
in winter, the cold didn't allow open doors so the
thick stained pine doors were closed.

"Let's get you inside," Flint said to Francis as
Honey stopped at the bottom of the church steps.
The sky had grown overcast and dark. There'd be
snow soon.

Flint swung his leg around awkwardly so he could
dismount before Francis and help her. Once on the
ground, Flint lifted his arms. "Just slide down. I've
got you."

"My leg's like wood," Francis whispered as she
leaned over.

Flint's heart would have stopped if it hadn't already been frozen. Thick rich waves of black hair
tumbled from her porcelain face, and the wedding
dress was cut to show off her curves.

How much torture can a man stand? Flint asked
himself as he clenched his jaw and did his duty. He
reached up, grabbed Francis by the waist and pulled
her off Honey. Flint almost welcomed the prickles

of icy pain that ran along his chest as Francis slid down him.

They were both freezing. Inside the church, the piano had begun to play an introduction to a hymn that sounded vaguely familiar. But outside, where they stood, snowflakes were beginning to fall.

"You just need to get your circulation back," Flint said soothingly, careful not to reveal either the tension that stretched inside him or his ever-increasing worry. At least they'd had snow boots and socks, so with luck they wouldn't have frostbite on their toes. "You'll be fine once we get you inside. Does that retired vet still go to church here?"

Voices inside, some off-key and some too loud, began to sing "Amazing Grace."

"Dr. Norris?" Francis tried to steady herself. A snowflake landed on her cheek. "I think so."

Flint hoped the vet was sitting inside right now. Francis relaxed her grip on his shoulders, and Flint could see she was trying to stand. She winced, and her face got even whiter than he'd thought possible. He needed to get her inside.

"Lean on me," Flint commanded. "Don't try to walk yourself."

"No," Francis protested. "I'll do it." She drew a breath of the frigid air to steady herself. "I take care of myself."

"Not while I'm around."

Flint didn't know where he got the strength. His

arms shot daggers of icy pain through him every time he moved them. His feet had gone numb long ago. But he could not bear to see Francis struggle. Flint bent his knees slightly and scooped Francis up in his arms.

"Oh," she breathed in surprise.

Flint shifted Francis so one hand was free to grab the railing that divided the cement steps. Francis hung around his neck as he pulled them both up the five stairs. He could as well have been climbing Mount Everest for the effort those five steps took. His legs were like frozen sausages, and that lace— Flint thought he'd never seen a wedding dress so full of lace. Layers of ivory froth were everywhere. They trailed between Flint's legs. They covered his arm. The bag of apples that Francis still clutched in her hand beat a gentle tap-tap on his back. Snow was falling everywhere.

Flint reached for the doorknob and tried to turn it. It was no good. His hand couldn't grasp it. He couldn't bend his fingers. He tried again. Finally, he gave the bottom of the door a thudding kick.

Please, God, let someone hear me.

The words to the second verse of "Amazing Grace" were filtering through the door. Someone was trilling a soprano harmony.

Flint kicked again.

The door slowly opened, and a young girl looked around it. She must be about seven, Flint thought.

She had serious eyes and short blond hair. Her eyes grew wide as she saw Flint and Francis.

"I thought it was Johnnie," she whispered. "He's the kind that'd kick at doors. You're not supposed to kick at doors," she added virtuously.

"I know. Can we come in?" Flint asked softly.

The girl nodded. "It's church. That's where brides are supposed to go."

The girl turned and opened the door wide.

Francis looked inside the church she'd visited often as a child. The walls were painted a light yellow, and thin sunshine streamed into the main room from tall rectangular windows of clear glass. The pews, made of solid oak over a hundred years ago, had an uneven patina because of the years of use. The church should look shabby, but it was too clean for that.

Today, the church was half full. Obviously the snow had kept some people away. But Francis looked and saw Mrs. Hargrove and the Edison family. Glory Beckett Curtis was there with the twin boys. Doris June was sharing a hymnal with a handsome man Francis didn't recognize.

The air inside the church was warm, and the faint hum of the heater could be heard from the doorway. Someone had fashioned a bouquet from pine boughs and holly branches and put it in front of the solid pulpit.

Everyone in the small church was looking at their hymnals, singing in unison.

We'll just slip into a back pew and whisper with the sheriff, Francis thought. *No need to disturb everyone.*

But Francis hadn't reckoned on the little girl.

"It's a wedding," the girl announced loudly as she opened both doors wide for Francis and Flint. "They need to get married."

Everything in the church stopped. Francis swore she heard a gasp, but maybe it was just the last note sung. The pianist stopped with her hands half-raised off the keyboard. Matthew Curtis, the minister who had been leading the singing, lifted his head and looked straight down the aisle at them. Every other head in the church slowly turned and looked at the open doorway.

Flint almost swore. Then he looked at Francis and saw what the citizens of Dry Creek saw at that very minute. Francis was all ivory and pink, with wet snowflakes like dewy sequins scattered over her face and arms. Ivory lace and netting spread out from her in luxuriant waves. The curls in her black hair had softened, and strands of her hair hung down, covering his hands. Flint had never believed in fairy-tale princesses until now. Francis was so beautiful he ached just looking at her. She was a bride.

Francis almost fainted. Then she looked at Flint's face and saw what the citizens of Dry Creek saw.

He was fierce and elegant all at the same time. The black silk of his tuxedo jacket fit his broad shoulders like it had been tailored for him. But his bare chest where his shirt had been—ah, Francis thought, she could see why the women looking their way were speechless. He looked more pirate than groom, but he looked every inch a man to be reckoned with.

"We're not—" she whispered.

"We don't—" he murmured.

But no one listened. There was a long, indrawn breath of silence, maybe even of awe, and then an eruption of joy.

"Congratulations!" someone yelled from the front pew.

"Hallelujah!" someone else shouted. "It's about time!"

And then everyone moved at once.

"Oh, your grandmother," Mrs. Hargrove said as she stepped out of her pew and started toward them, dabbing a handkerchief at her eyes. "If she could have only lived to see—" She looked at the ceiling. "Or are you watching, Essie?"

The pianist's hands went to the keyboard, only now they were playing, "Here Comes the Bride."

Francis felt the gentle hands of two young girls touching her dress reverently.

"We're not," Flint tried again.

"We don't," Francis tried, joining him.

"Why doesn't anyone tell me anything?" Sheriff

Wall complained as he slipped out of the last pew and walked toward them. "If I'd know you were planning this, I'd have brought my marrying book."

"I've got my book," Matthew Curtis said, smiling widely from the front of the aisle. "What a great way to start a Sunday morning! A surprise wedding!"

Flint felt the twinge in his stomach grow into a knot. He'd been scared when old man Gossett pointed that gun at him. He'd thought he was a goner when the old man left him and Francis to freeze to death. But nothing—absolutely none of it—terrified him like this moment.

He knew now why he'd asked Francis to elope twenty years ago. That was all he had the courage for. Some quick marriage in Vegas had none of the glow that standing in this church in wedding clothes had. The good people of Dry Creek stood around him, and he was almost undone by the expectation he saw on their faces. They expected something from him—something good, something important, something lasting.

He, Flint Harris, did not have the grit to face that kind of responsibility. It was beyond him. He couldn't bear to disappoint everyone, and he was sure to fail.

Francis felt the joy leave her. For a moment, she'd been caught up in the dream. Maybe, just maybe she and Flint would go along with the enthusiasm of those around them. They'd be married—truly, gloriously married—finally.

Then Francis had looked up and seen the change in Flint's face. If she hadn't known him so well, she wouldn't have seen it at all. His jaw had tightened—not much, it was true, but enough. His eyes got a hunted look in them and grew hooded, like he wanted to hide his feelings. He was smiling, but it was only a motion of his lips.

He doesn't want to marry me, Francis thought dully. *He doesn't want to be impolite—to embarrass me in front of all of these people—but he clearly doesn't want to marry me.*

"There's been a misunderstanding," Francis said calmly. Strange how the cold that had nearly frozen her earlier hadn't touched her heart the way the cold in Flint's eyes did now. She nudged Flint, and he opened his arms so that she could slide to the floor and stand alone. She was, after all, alone. No sense pretending otherwise. "The clothes—they're not ours—"

The church went silent once again.

"Old man Gossett has kidnapped Robert and Jenny and is making them fly him into Billings."

"Why, the old coot," Mrs. Hargrove said indignantly. "Doesn't he know that's dangerous? It's already starting to snow again."

"I don't think he cares," Francis continued. "He

has two guns and he wanted to meet some bus in Billings.''

"Where's he got to go that's so all-fired important?" someone muttered.

Flint met the inspector's eyes. The inspector had been in the last pew, as they had agreed earlier, and the pew had been roped off with a gold cord, waiting for Francis to arrive.

"He's our man?" the inspector asked Flint quietly. "The informant?"

Flint nodded. "We'd better alert the police in Billings to pick him up at the airport. He's running."

"Armed and dangerous?" Sheriff Wall stepped closer to Flint. "I'll put out an APB."

Francis felt soft hands tugging at her dress. She looked into the face of the young girl.

"You're still a bride, aren't you?" the little girl asked, worried. "You're wearing a bride's dress."

"A dress doesn't make a bride," Francis answered softly.

"But the dress is the best part of the wedding," the little girl said, confident in her knowledge. "Except for the cake, maybe. Does this mean there's no cake, either?"

The girl's mother appeared at her side, "Hush, now, don't bother Francis with your questions."

"It's no bother," Francis said woodenly as she made an effort to smile at the girl. "And I wish there was a cake— I love wedding cake, too."

When Francis looked up from the girl, she noticed that Flint had gone to talk with the inspector and the sheriff. They were standing in the back pew muttering, and the inspector had his cell phone in his hand.

Flint had already borrowed a parka from the inspector and had replaced the tuxedo jacket with it. He hadn't wasted any time getting back to normal, Francis thought, as she let Mrs. Hargrove lead her to a pew so she could sit.

"Such a pity," Mrs. Hargrove muttered as she settled Francis in a pew and tucked her coat around Francis's shoulders.

Francis didn't know whether the older woman was talking about Mr. Gossett or the wedding that didn't happen, but she didn't ask.

Chapter Thirteen

Flint spit, then drove another nail into the side boards on his grandmother's house. The air was cold, and he felt a bitter satisfaction with the way the frigid air caught in his throat. The board didn't need that nail. It hadn't needed the other ten he drove in before it, either. But it was hammer or go crazy, and so he kept his hand curled around the tool and his mind focused on the nail. The solid blows of iron on iron suited him.

He sank that nail deep and pulled another one out of his shirt pocket. He had it positioned ready for striking when he heard the sound of a Jeep pulling itself up the slight incline that led to his grandmother's old house.

House, nothing, he said to himself as he looked at the weathered boards. The old thing could hardly be called a house anymore. It was more shack than house at the moment. When the windows had broken out, the snow and rain of twenty-some years had broken down the interior.

It would need to be gutted, he thought. A new roof and gutted.

The driver of the Jeep honked the horn as the vehicle slowed to a stop in front of the house.

Flint didn't want company. He'd already had a dozen congratulatory calls on his cell phone, telling him he was brilliant for figuring out that Mr. Gossett had changed his mind a second time and asked Robert fly him to Fargo, after all. Flint had cut all the calls short.

Flint knew he wasn't brilliant. It didn't take brilliance to know what a cornered animal would do when you felt like you were one yourself.

Flint hit the nail square and grunted. He wondered how many nails he'd have to hit before he felt human again.

"There you are." Mrs. Hargrove's cheery voice came from behind him.

If it had been anyone else, Flint would have asked them to leave. Since it was his grandmother's dearest friend, he only grunted and hit the nail again. He hoped she'd take the hint. She didn't.

"I brought you some oatmeal cookies," she continued. "I remember how you used to like them."

Flint had no choice but to turn and smile at the woman. "Thanks. I appreciate that."

"I thought you might be out here," she mused as she set a small box down and wiped the snow off the top porch step, Then she eased herself down and unwound the wool scarf she wore around her head. "Never can hear with that scarf on."

Flint had a sinking feeling that meant she was going to expect conversation. "I'm fixing the side wall here."

Mrs. Hargrove nodded and was silent.

"Thought I'd put some windows in, too." Flint went on. Her sitting there silent made him nervous. "Maybe fix that leak in the roof."

"Essie would like that," Mrs. Hargrove finally said. "You living here."

"Me? Live here? No, I'm just fixing it up."

Mrs. Hargrove nodded. "You're going to sell it then?"

"Sell it? I couldn't do that—it's Grandmother's house."

Mrs. Hargrove was silent so long that Flint positioned another nail and hit it.

"Essie doesn't need the house anymore, you know," Mrs. Hargrove finally said gently. "You don't have to take care of it for her."

"She wouldn't like it if it was run down."

"She wouldn't blame you for it if it was."

"I wouldn't want to disappoint her," Flint said

softly as he gripped the hammer and hit the nail again. "I've disappointed enough folks as it is."

"Essie was never disappointed in you."

"She should have been— I messed up enough times."

"Everybody messes up sometimes," Mrs. Hargrove said softly. "Your grandmother knew that— She was a big believer in grace and forgiveness."

Flint grunted. "My grandmother was a saint."

Mrs. Hargrove chuckled. "Not to hear her tell it. She used to say the vein of guilt that ran through your family was thick enough to make somebody rich if they could only mine it."

Flint looked up for the first time. "But she never failed anyone. She was as close to perfect as anyone could be. What did she ever need forgiveness for?"

"We all need forgiveness," Mrs. Hargrove said softly as she placed a motherly hand on Flint's arm. "We all fall short somewhere or other. But we can't let it stop us or we'd never—" Mrs. Hargrove stopped abruptly. "Why, that's it! That's why you're out here pounding away at those rusty old nails instead of sweet-talking Francis! You're afraid."

Flint winced. "I wouldn't say that."

"And just what would you say, then?"

Flint grimaced. "I'm cautious—based on my knowledge of myself, I'm cautious about promising something and then disappointing someone."

"You don't love her, then?"

Flint squirmed. "No, that's not the problem."

"You intend to marry her and then leave her someday and break her heart?"

"Why, no, of course not, I wouldn't do that."

Flint wondered if it would be too impolite to climb on the roof and take care of those loose shingles while he was thinking about them. Mrs. Hargrove had the tenacity of a bulldog.

"Well, son, what is it that's eating away at you then?"

"I need to fix the roof."

"And that's why you can't get married?" she asked incredulously.

Flint sighed. There was no way out of this one but to go through the scorching fire. "I'm just not good enough, all right? Somewhere, sometime, I'd let her down. I'd forget her birthday. I don't make jelly, you know. Never learned how."

Mrs. Hargrove looked at him blankly.

"Even old man Gossett has a cellar full of crab-apple jelly. He must be able to make it. Me, I can't even make a company cup of coffee—what kind of a husband would I make?"

Mrs. Hargrove didn't say anything.

"Besides, I've noticed some thinning in my hair. I could go bald someday."

"Your hair looks fine to me," Mrs. Hargrove interrupted skeptically.

"That's not the point," Flint said in exasperation.

"It's just an example of what could happen, and anything could happen."

Mrs. Hargrove eyed him thoughtfully. "You don't have a clue about grace and forgiveness, do you? And after all those Bible verses I taught you in Sunday school, I would have thought one or two would stick."

"They did stick," Flint said softly. "It's just that being forgiven by God isn't quite the same as being forgiven by a flesh-and-blood wife you've disappointed."

Mrs. Hargrove snorted. "You can't fool me. You don't remember them, after all, do you? Recite me one."

"Now?"

Mrs. Hargrove nodded.

Flint's mind scrambled. "I remember one about four times forty—or was it eight times eighty?"

"Seven times seventy." Mrs. Hargrove shook her head. "That's how many times we're to forgive someone." She fixed him with a challenging eye. "Do you figure you'll mess up more times than that? That's almost five hundred times. Francis isn't likely to have nearly that many birthdays."

"Well, there'd be anniversaries, too. Every year April seventeenth will roll around—"

"Surely you're not planning to forget them all?" Mrs. Hargrove demanded. "Give yourself some credit."

Flint stopped in the middle of a swing with the hammer. He knew he wouldn't forget the anniversaries. He hadn't forgotten one of them yet. "I might not need to worry about the anniversaries."

Mrs. Hargrove nodded complacently. "They've been a sore spot, have they?"

Flint looked at her indignantly. How did she know these things?

The older woman laughed. "You're a Harris. None of the folks in your family ever took lightly to love. Essie used to say it gave everyone another reason to suffer."

Flint grunted and then admitted slowly, "I've hated April for years. The first five anniversaries I went out and got stinking drunk on April seventeenth, and then sat down and wrote a scathing letter to Francis." He smiled. "I wrote down all my disappointments for the whole year like they were all her fault. Finally, I was able to tell her the good things, too—and how I missed her."

Flint concentrated on steadying another nail.

"Well, if you remembered your anniversary for years, what makes you think you'd forget it if Francis were with you?"

Flint didn't know. That was what had been gnawing at him for the past two days. He didn't know why he was so nervous about taking a flying leap into matrimony, he just knew that he was.

"You need to sit down with Essie's Bible," Mrs. Hargrove declared. "Maybe then you can make some sense out of yourself."

"Yes, ma'am."

The older woman eased herself off the porch and stood. "Remember, this is lightning country." She nodded at the nails in the piece of board. "Much more of that and this place will catch the next bolt that comes flying through."

Flint smiled. He wasn't so sure the bolt wasn't already here. "Thanks for stopping by."

"Just see to your reading."

Flint had no intention of reading the Bible, but he felt almost like he'd promised. And so he opened it after Mrs. Hargrove had left and began to read the verses his grandmother had highlighted. The afternoon slipped into dusk and the sun was going down before he realized he'd spent the afternoon looking for the answers to the gnawing inside himself.

When he realized what time it was, he pulled out his cell phone and made a call to the manager of his apartment building.

"Yes, I'd like you to send them overnight express." He finished his instructions. "I'll go into Miles City tomorrow and get them."

Francis was standing in the small bedroom she used at Garth's house. She was packing. Her old-fashioned suitcase was open on the bed. It was a good-quality suitcase, but it had none of the modern pockets and compartments. Francis always maintained that a neat person didn't need to fear packing and certainly didn't need compartments.

Francis's socks were neatly paired and folded with the toes under. Her bras were folded and laid conveniently close to her panty hose. She had loose tissue to pack around her slacks and two dresses. Organizing her clothes made her feel like there was something in her life she could control just the way she wanted it. She might not be good with men, but she was good with avoiding creases.

Francis had waited around for Flint Harris once before, and she couldn't bear to do it again. Flint's face had been cold when she'd last seen him three days ago, and it had nothing to do with the weather. Sam was getting restless and wanted her to fly back to Denver with him. She'd told him she'd be ready tomorrow. He might be a little dull, but Sam was a good man.

"You're leaving?"

The deep voice came from the doorway to the small bedroom, and Francis whirled.

"Who let you in?" Francis swore she'd fry the culprit in hot oil.

"Garth," Flint said simply. "He told me I have five minutes."

"That's five more than I would have given you."

Flint had his outdoor parka on, and there were flecks of snow melting on his shoulders. He might have had a hat on his head, because his hair was slightly rumpled. He was fresh-shaven, and his hands held a small plastic bag with the name of a Miles City drugstore stamped on it.

Flint nodded seriously. "I figured as much, and you don't even know the half of it." He hesitated and took a deep breath. "I have a drawer full of mismatched socks in my apartment, and baldness runs in my family."

Francis looked at him in astonishment.

Flint nodded glumly. "It's true. One of my mother's brothers. That's the worst odds, they say. And I don't know how to make jelly—or really good coffee—I guess I could maybe manage a cup of tea and dry toast—"

"What in the world are you talking about?"

"I've had to kill two men. They were evil men and I had to do it, but it's there all the same—plus I work too much." Flint staunchly continued his list. "Although I have been thinking about chickens for the last day or so, and maybe it's time to quit my job and take them on. I've made good investments over the years so money's not a problem. It'd work out."

Francis was becoming worried. "Did Dr. Norris check you out when we got back to Dry Creek? I've heard of sunstroke doing this to people, but maybe extreme cold acts in the same way—''

"Of course, if you don't still want to do chickens, we could try our hand at something else." Flint cleared his throat and continued his speech. He didn't want to get derailed. If he did, he might not get back on the track again. "I've decided I like Dry Creek. I like the church here and I think that's going to be important to me. And the air is good. Hard to get good air anymore."

Francis looked at Flint. His eyes looked clear enough to swim in, and he didn't have any strange twitches happening with his mouth. Then she remembered the drugstore bag he carried.

"Is that medicine you have with you?" she asked gently. Maybe that's why she hadn't heard from him for three days. "You poor man."

Francis stepped to Flint and placed her hand on his forehead. "Did Dr. Norris give you something to take?"

Flint's mouth went dry. His voice croaked. "I'm not sick." Flint swore no man in the history of the world had bungled a job like he was doing.

"Of course you are," Francis said softly. "What else could this be?"

Flint took a deep breath and plunged. "It could be a marriage proposal."

Francis stared at him, her hand frozen on his cheek.

"Not a good proposal, I'll admit," Flint continued shakily. "But I thought you should know the problems up front. I've always believed in saying the truth straight out."

"Marriage?" Francis's voice squeaked. "But the medicine?"

"It's not medicine," Flint said softly. "It's cards—for you."

Francis looked around for support and sat on the bed.

Flint opened the bag and held up twenty envelopes. Some of the envelopes were white. Some pink. A few ivory. One even had pale green stripes on it. Each one had the number of a year written on it in black ink.

"They're anniversary cards," Flint said softly as he fanned them out on the bed next to her. "Bought the whole store out. One for each year—and inside is the letter I wrote you in that year."

"You wrote me?" Francis whispered.

Flint nodded. "I had to."

"Oh." Francis brushed a tear from her eye. She tried to focus, to think this new information through, but for once in her life she didn't care about the order of anything. "I thought you'd forgotten me."

"How could I forget the only woman I've ever loved?" Flint said softly. The tears gave him hope. He would carry this through in any event, but the tears did give him hope.

Flint pulled a long-stemmed yellow rose out of an inner pocket in his parka. It was the only yellow rose to be had in Miles City, and it was a little peaked. Then he dropped to one knee and offered the rose to Francis. "Will you marry me again? This time for good?"

"Oh." Francis swallowed.

"Is that an 'oh, yes' or an 'oh, no'?" Flint asked quietly.

"Yes," she stammered. "My, yes. It's an 'oh, yes.'"

Flint reached up and brushed the tears from her eyes before he leaned forward and kissed her. The pure sweetness of it sang inside of him. He didn't deserve someone like Francis.

"I could maybe do something about those socks."

Francis laughed and touched his cheek. Yes, he was real. "I don't care about the socks."

"This time let's get married in the church here in front of everyone in Dry Creek," Flint said. "I want to see my bride walk down that aisle."

Francis smiled dreamily. "Dry Creek does love a bride."

"Not half as much as I do," Flint said, smiling as he bent his head to kiss Francis again. "Not half as much as I do."

* * * * *

Dear Reader,

I should have my mother write you this note. She, having raised five usually wonderful children (of which I am blessed to be one), knows far more of the hope that goes into love than I do. Actually, most mothers know that kind of hope—the hope that their love will bear fruit, that their love will ease someone's pain and that it will even give that person an anchor in life.

Love laced with hope is a useful kind of love. It sees beyond the romantic parts of love and looks to the future.

That's why, when I chose to tell the story of Francis, I knew it had to be a story of hope. We never know when we love someone what our hopes will bring. Francis did not know. Flint did not know. Only God knew.

May this story of Francis and Flint encourage you to love with hope and to trust God for a happy ending.

Janet Tronstad

Next month from
Steeple Hill's

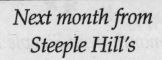
Love Inspired

SECOND CHANCES
by

Valerie Hansen

Belinda Carnes could hardly believe it!
Paul Randall was back in town. Though
they had been torn apart by her
disapproving father, Belinda had never
stopped loving the bad boy with the
good heart. Now, ten years later, Paul
was a successful lawyer with a bright
future—and still in love with Belinda. But
could he convince her that God had
given them a second chance for love?

**Don't miss
SECOND CHANCES
On sale June 2001**

Love Inspired

Next month from Steeple Hill's

Love Inspired®

CASSANDRA'S SONG

by

Carole Gift Page

Cassandra Rowland never thought she would fall in love—until she met Antonio Pagliarulo! The concert singer enthralled Cassandra with his dazzling tenor voice and gentlemanly manner. Would she set aside her reluctance and trust that God would guide her to the love of a lifetime?

**Don't miss
CASSANDRA'S SONG
On sale June 2001**

Love Inspired®